GOD MODE

———

A novel by
TESLA TAO

DIM SUM BOOKS
NEW YORK

DIM SUM BOOKS PRINT EDITION, OCTOBER 2012

Text Copyright © 2012 Tesla Tao.

DIM SUM BOOKS PRINT ISBN: 978-0-9859927-1-2

www.teslatao.com
Dim Sum Books / New York, New York
Cover design: Lana Redgrove
Main cover image: Bruce Rolff

Printed in the United States of America

For my family

CHAPTER 1

Trey Hedges was terrified—as intended.

After all, if his neurons didn't signal fear, then standing on the bridge—with what felt like fifty pounds of bungee cords lashed around his ankles—would've been pointless.

That was his left-brain talking. Cool ... analytical.

But the 25-year-old quantum physicist's right-brain was in the driver's seat for a change, controlling his cortical emotion center, and the FEAR pedal was jammed all the way down. It had to be.

They needed his neurons to be electrified; if he hadn't been terrified of heights, the bungee scene would belong to another section of the immersion menu—the PLEASURE category perhaps. But they'd already recorded PLEASURE, back in Paris. Today's category was FEAR.

I'll take FEAR for six hundred, Alex.

"Kid, quit bein' a sissy and get on with it ... I'd like to get back to the jet before I'm sixty."

His back stiffened when he heard the all-too-familiar drawl and he glanced at his boss, who was standing next to the bungee attendant.

Derrick Pierce: recluse, eccentric billionaire, ersatz leader of the free world. The man his right-brain blamed for his predicament.

Pierce smirked and lit one of his foul cigars. Overdressed for the day's itinerary, he wore his usual uniform of a custom-tailored suit and ratty, old cowboy boots.

Hedges looked away from the Director of Pantheon Holdings; he'd seen enough of him during their recording tour, besides—for once—Derrick Pierce wasn't his primary concern.

His eyes shifted to the weathered sign that heralded his fate: BUNGEE SOUTH AFRICA! GUINNESS WORLDS RECORDS HIGHEST COMMERCIAL BRIDGE JUMP – 700 FEET ABOVE THE BLOUKRANS RIVER!

The reminder of the height was bad enough, but the cord around his ankles

(a single cord for your freefalling pleasure!)

was a major concern and again he wondered how it would keep his head from smashing into the river rocks below.

His left-brain, unaccustomed to being idle, jumped in to calculate the energy equation for the jump: maximum load, pounds force per foot, his mass, the length of the cord, potential energy, kinetic—

Don't look down!

His right-brain interrupted the calculation with a timely reminder, but Hedges didn't look down. He'd been careful not to.

Instead, he stared ahead, chin up, but the new view wasn't much better. Now, all he saw was how the bungee operation seemed designed to bring to mind the gallows.

Hedges wondered if bungee jump designers paid as much attention to the user experience as did interface designers back at the Agrippa Research Complex. The ones back home in Virginia....

As he looked at the bridge, at the shape of the structure, he realized he must be looking at a UIX designer's interpretation of jump psychology.

He envisioned a team, sitting around, poring over a schematic, and saying: "But if we make the platform look more like a trapdoor and the cord look like a noose ... oh, and while we're at it, we should hire attendants who resemble only the most disinterested executioners, then, I think we'll give our users a memorable experience!"

Well done guys, Hedges thought. Spot on. And, somehow, just barely, he managed to keep from glancing down to see if there were—indeed—trapdoor hinges at his feet.

But he knew there weren't.

He knew without looking there were red arrows—scuffed and faded—painted on the slats. They pointed toward the edge of the bridge. After the arrows, there were two red footprints toed to a red line. Beyond the line, was—

Enough! We know what's beyond the red line.

His head started to buzz and he knew if he didn't focus on something else, he'd lose it. So, he tried to concentrate on the task at hand, the reason for being there: to record FEAR.

Fear was the final sensation to be added to their immersion packet, and the implant in his brain was rarin' to go. The red light blinked inside his right eye, ready to capture every terrifying detail.

As Hedges faced the seven hundred-foot death-drop, he reflected on his life choices.

True, he got to work with the best and latest technology at Pantheon, got to work on quantum cryptography detection. More important, he had exclusive access to a multibillion-dollar, ionospheric collector array—the technology that had led to their discovery of the Grid beacon....

But, was it worth it, he wondered, knowing what he knew now—about Pierce's intentions— would he still have taken the job?

Hedges knew the answer—the Grid was worth almost any sacrifice. He only hoped he'd be able to share it with the rest of the world. But, his boss had other ideas, and Derrick Pierce usually got what he wanted—

At that moment, the attendant stepped forward and motioned to Hedges, indicating he should move toward the red footsteps ... toward the line at the edge of the bridge.

4

It was time to capture fear sensations for the enjoyment of all beings of the Universe....

Hedges took a deep breath, kept his chin up, kept his eyes from dropping down, straightened to his full height and, with resolve, activated the implant.

Record, he thought, and the red light turned green.

Then, he hobbled forward, closer to the red line, and did the one thing he'd warned himself not to do. He looked down.

HolyMaryMotherofGod!

Every image he'd been trying to shut out came flooding in. The arrows leading to the edge, the red footprints, the green and yellow treetops far below and the jagged river rocks that peeked through the foliage, here and there. His fingers tingled and his heartbeat slowed ... and it was hot! He was suddenly burning up. His blood thumped, slow and lazy in his head, and everything seemed to empty out up there giving him the sensation of lightness ... *so dizzy*. The bridge edge pulsed in and out of focus and the green light in the corner of his eye blinked and blurred ... off to the side, he saw Pierce's lips move but he couldn't make out the words; they were slow, muffled and seemed to be coming from far away. Everything darkened then, fading like the dimming of a monitor screen *(must be a storm cloud coming)* fading in from the corners until there was just a pinpoint—

CHAPTER 2

The limp mass that was Hedges—the six-foot-four, one hundred and ninety pound bag of bone and tissue, with a cord wrapped around one end— folded toward the edge of the platform.

Without missing a beat, the attendant reached out, grabbed Hedges's harness and yanked him back like a wayward dog, back to the red line.

The force of being jerked back revived Hedges; he stood, tottering on the platform, dizzy and disoriented. At first, he didn't know where he was; in his mind, everything had smeared into a jetlagged blur of different cities, different continents, different tourist attractions.

But then he saw everything—Pierce, the attendant, the gallows—and realized he was back in South Africa, back above the Bloukrans River. Back in his own fresh hell.

And, inside the corner of his eye, the blinking green light mocked him; the implant recorder hadn't missed a beat.

Well, Hedges thought, at least Grid users will get to feel the sensation of fainting on Earth, but that'll have to be the extent of it....

"I'm not doing this." Shaking and feeling the need to vomit, he hobbled around and shuffled, oh so carefully, away from the edge. He shuffled past the red footsteps, toward the red arrows.

With his ankles bound, he wavered and teetered, like a lone figure at the start of a 700-foot-high, three-legged race.

Pierce looked at him, disgusted and annoyed. The attendant looked bored. The guy had probably seen it all; Hedges was sure he wasn't the first to chicken out.

The three stood on the bridge and, for a moment, all was calm.

The wind had died down. It was warm, but not too warm—a pleasant, early-October day in South Africa—and Hedges could see the shadows lengthening in the mid-day sun. The bungee platform smelled of cigars, nylon cords, and the axle grease that was slathered on the cord winch—the one Hedges was tethered to. The winch standing by to haul up the fresh catch-of-the-day....

Pierce regarded Hedges through narrowed eyes and a shadow passed over his face. Then he smiled and drawled, "All right, kid, if you can't do it, you can't do it."

He popped the cigar between his teeth to free his hands for other things and advanced toward Hedges, as if to help. As if to help him away from the edge, from the brink—as if to pull him to safety.

As if to say: "Everything's fine, shit howdy! Of course I'll help you get the noose off and we'll mosey on back to the jet, back to Virginia, back to the Ops Center. Back to the Grid room, where there are only ion traps and quantum hoohah ... back to where there are no red footprints and no trapdoor hinges."

And—probably because Logic and Reason were still on hiatus, *on a little vaycay*—Hedges *believed* Pierce intended to free him from the bungee cord.

But, as Pierce advanced, smiling benignly, Hedges saw *the look* in the Director's eyes. It was the look he got every time Hedges asked when the PIT beta test would be over. When he asked when they could tell the rest of the world about what Pantheon had found....

Pierce would get *the look* and would say: *"Soon, we're very close."* But now, Hedges knew better. He knew what that look meant, and seeing it up on the bridge was not a good omen. Not at all.

So Hedges backed away—*backed away!*—from Pierce because the look was so alarming and because he'd forgotten how close he was to a 700-foot drop.

It happened fast: too fast this time, for the attendant to intervene....

It didn't take much to push Hedges off the bridge; he was already off-balance, already teetering, so Pierce needed only to tap on Hedges's chest, just above the harness straps—like he was pushing on a fence post to see if it was solidly in the hole—and Hedges fell *backward* off the bridge.

The first things he saw after his feet left solid ground—what he saw through the sharp lens of terror—were Pierce's cowboy boots, half-covering red footprints. Then, he saw Pierce's look of dispassionate examination—the same look he'd seen in Johnny Palecki's eyes when Johnny had held the magnifying glass to catch the rays of the sun, to focus them into a hot laser point on the kitten's neck.

Hedges tore his eyes from Pierce's and shifted his gaze to the Bloukrans Bridge. There, he saw the metal underside he'd soon see—up-close and personal—when his head smashed into it after the bungee cord bounced him back up like some man-sized Yo-Yo....

As he sped toward the river below, he felt every sensation, magnified by a factor of a thousand and the screams of the kitten were the worst of all.

But in the middle of his free fall, halfway down, Hedges realized, he was the one screaming.

CHAPTER 3

Derrick Pierce swirled the whiskey in his glass and settled deeper into the soft, buttery leather of the custom-designed couch. He was on Pantheon-III, the latest addition to his jet fleet.

The jet was a pre-release model from the 2016 JetLaunch Supersonic Business line, the first personal aircraft capable of Mach 2.5. At the moment, however, the display on the table in front of him—the one next to the ashtray—indicated they were cruising at Mach 2.0.

The display also told him they'd be in Virginia in less than half an hour.

This jet—even though it was produced by one of Branson Ross's companies—was his favorite so far.

Branson may be all hat 'n no cattle in some areas, but the lily-livered liberal *did* know how to build a fine plane. If the guy focused his energies on the aviation and aerospace industries, and stayed out of personal tech and military intelligence, things might go smoother for everyone.

Several weeks ago, Pierce had struggled with whether or not to invite Branson to become a PIT user, but in the end, decided it would be worth it for bragging rights alone. He was happy he had, particularly when his plan evolved. And hell, rubbin' Branson's nose in it was a bonus.

Pierce tugged at his shirt cuffs, picked up his cigar, and smiled. Now that Earth's immersion packet was recorded, he was closer than ever to his goal.

Over the weekend, the kid would edit their packet, convert it into quantum-hoohah, then send it on up. Then, finally, Earth would be granted full Grid access, but more important, the tech library would be unlocked.

Pierce thought again of the file, with its grayed out font and padlock icon that taunted and teased....

The only way to get at the library was to go through the time and expense of recording their packet and submitting it to the Grid for approval. But that didn't mean that, once they got it unlocked, they'd have to continue to cater to the Grid's rules ... to cater to their open-sharing twaddle.

Who would've guessed an alien internet would be run like some la-dee-da, daisy-chain-makin' commune?

The sound of the kid's snoring interrupted his thoughts.

He looked over at Trey Hedges, who was sacked out on the crescent-shaped couch on the other side of the plane.

Back when Pierce had met him for the final interview, he'd thought the headhunter had sent him the wrong candidate. Hedges was so unlike the awkward and gawky nerdlets of Agrippa. He was tall, with an athletic build, clean cut, with sandy brown hair.

Pierce puffed on his cigar and narrowed his eyes, studying the kid through the yellow-brown haze. Even though he'd put up with a passel of whining during their recording tour—particularly on the bridge in South Africa—for the most part, Hedges had been tolerable.

According to HR, the kid's IQ was higher than any they'd ever tested—with one exception. And when the smarter nerdlet turned the job down, Pierce gave it to Hedges.

A good choice, as it turned out; the kid's invention had found the Grid.

But—several days prior—the kid had made it clear he didn't agree with Pierce's decision to keep the tech library classified. So now, he needed to keep Hedges under tighter surveillance than usual. Nothing could jeopardize Monday's activities.

Monday was Tech Day.

CHAPTER 4

Saturday, October 3, 2015
Agrippa Research Complex
Pantheon Headquarters: Building Q

Marvin Trimble, with the Cerulean immersion fresh in his mind, was unaware that, by morning, he'd be dead.

The diminutive human resources director remained reclined in the chair, eyes closed. Although his neural implant had reached the end of the immersion, he wanted to retain—for as long as possible—what it had felt like to be tall.

He'd chosen the packet because, in addition to having the ability to perceive the entire electromagnetic spectrum, Ceruleans were, on average, about eight feet tall.

And, as he'd moved through the landscape, he'd felt normal for the first time in his life, hadn't felt self-conscious about his height. He was at eye-level with every native he encountered and—until the immersion—he hadn't realized how infrequently that happened ... on Earth.

Marvin sighed and opened his eyes. He reoriented himself to his surroundings—a Planet

Immersion Travel room hidden below Pantheon headquarters.

The room reminded him of a treatment room at the Luxist Spa, in D.C.: small and cozy, with low lighting and muted wall colors, but thankfully, without the New Age music and froufrou, scented candles.

He was reclined in a comfortable, salon-style chair. He was short—5 feet 4 inches—so there was still plenty of chair extending beyond his outstretched legs.

Hanging several feet above, the Onculus waited, its gray arm folded like a swinging lamp, ready to be lowered, ready to retrieve the Cerulean packet. But, instead of a lamp at the end of the arm, there was an eye-shaped, silicon suction cup.

Marvin turned his head and looked at the Onculus control panel. It was a small touchscreen jutting from the left arm of the chair.

He tapped at the START icon and heard a *click* and a *whir* as the arm straightened and lowered. The suction cup stopped a few inches from his right eye.

He reached over, tapped on the RETRIEVE icon and white text appeared in the air, next to the Onculus arm.

CONFIRM PACKET RETRIEVAL?

He hesitated.

This part always made him nervous. Even though Hedges had explained that the Onculus technology was safe—that it had been used throughout the Universe for billions of years— Marvin was leery of the deposit and retrieval process.

After all, the technology had only been used on Earth for the last several months. What if the contractors made an error when interpreting the Onculus build diagrams and schematics, the ones received from the Grid?

Geniuses *could* make mistakes, couldn't they?

Marvin was just an MBA ... just a simple HR guy. He wasn't like the legions of wunderkinds roving Agrippa. Not like the Ph.D.s, mathematicians, physicists, and engineers. *They'd* know the science behind the whole PIT system and would be comforted by the knowledge.

But for Marvin, no matter how patiently the Onculus design was explained, it still seemed like so much smoke and mirrors—like magic.

It was only *after* immersion that his unease threatened to overtake him. It was easier to push past the fear before packet download—before an immersion—because his desire to travel within an alien landscape for an hour, was stronger than his fear of the Onculus. But now that the trip was over, Marvin procrastinated before giving the retrieval command.

Finally, he got on with it and tapped at the CONFIRM icon.

The Onculus arm lowered the rest of the way until the suction cup rested on his right eye. Then, a laser scanned his retina. It locked onto his implant, located the Cerulean immersion packet, and the retrieval process began.

As the packet was removed—*neural*bit by *neural*bit—the pressure in his brain subsided. In the corner of his eye, a progress indicator showed the amount of data retrieved.

85%

Suddenly, in a deviation from past retrievals, the laser stopped. The indicator read 95%.

Marvin waited, expecting the laser to start again. But it didn't.

Instead, the pressure on his eye—the pressure from the suction cup—eased, and the Onculus began to retract.

He jabbed at the touchpad, at the RETRIEVE icon, but the Onculus continued to retract until it had returned to its fully folded position against the ceiling. Then, another message appeared.

RETRIEVAL FAILURE: 5%

Stunned, Marvin stared at the message, wondering what he'd done wrong.

He glanced around the room and wondered if they were watching. He ignored the voice in his head, the one warning him to report the issue; Marvin—like everyone else—tried to stay clear of Derrick Pierce's radar.

So, in a lapse of judgment, he fled the PIT room, fled the underground, and prayed the incident would go unnoticed.

CHAPTER 5

After a fitful night's sleep, Hedges awoke in unfamiliar surroundings.

Groggy, he rubbed his eyes and glanced around, expecting to see the interior of a five-star hotel room. Another like the one in South Africa or the one at the George V in Paris.

But he wasn't in a hotel room. These accommodations were much more austere. Drab. Functional.

He was back in the United States, back in Northern Virginia, but he wasn't in his own bedroom. He was in the Pantheon barracks. He'd heard the rumors about an underground emergency bunker—one built by the Crazy Cowboy as some sort of doomsday shelter—but he'd never believed it.

It was like a studio apartment with a bed, a small dining table, a bathroom, a kitchenette, and an open pantry stockpiled with emergency rations.

There were stacks of canned food, cases of bottled water, and several tiers of those white, survival food buckets he thought only loons and conspiracy theorists bought.

His saw his luggage, dumped just inside the door, and the events of the night before came flooding back.

After they'd landed at Pierce's private airstrip, they were chauffeured to the Agrippa Research Complex. In Building Q, they'd gone underground, but instead of stopping at the PITs, they had continued on. Judging from the travel time in the sideways elevator, Hedges estimated he was underneath Building A.

The most disturbing thing, apart from being locked up, was what he'd seen as they walked from the elevator to the studio: rows and rows of what looked like half-finished PIT rooms, most empty, but, some with Onculus fittings and chairs.

Unlike the chairs in the functional PIT rooms, these had restraints.

When Hedges asked about the rooms, asked what they'd been used for, Pierce was silent. He locked Hedges in, saying security would escort him out in the morning: his pheromone signature would be deactivated, just to be safe.

Pierce said he was doing it for the good of the project, to be sure there were no security leaks, but Hedges suspected he was being punished for telling his boss how he felt about keeping the tech library classified.

Hedges still couldn't believe what Pierce intended to do. Once Earth's immersion packet was uploaded to the Grid and the tech library was unlocked, Pierce said he'd keep the tech classified. Would keep—hidden from humanity—the billions of years of technological advancements invented by intelligent life forms throughout the cosmos. He intended to cherry-pick those he deemed useful.

He'd file patents and have his global network of contractors produce and manufacture the tech, all the while letting the world believe the inventions originated from Pierce, from Pantheon.

When Hedges reminded Pierce that blocking Earth's users from any part of the Grid was a violation of its open sharing policy—that doing so would result in the permanent revocation of Earth's access—Pierce waved it away as though it were inconsequential. He'd said: "So what? Once the tech library is open, I'll have everything I need."

Hedges couldn't understand how Pierce didn't see the value in the Grid's cooperative sharing. How could the self-proclaimed visionary be so shortsighted?

But, if he was honest with himself, he'd have to admit he'd known all along that Pierce never meant to share the Grid with the rest of the world. It wasn't in his nature—

His thoughts were interrupted by a knock on the door. Then, he heard the metallic scrape of a key in the lock.

The door swung open, its hinges creaking from disuse, and Reggie, Pantheon's senior security officer, poked his head in. "Get dressed. There's been a system alert."

CHAPTER 6

Click.

COMM: DPIERCE.

"Sir, there's been a QUINN alert."

"Whatdya mean?"

"From PIT-2 … after Marvin Trimble's trip."

"And?"

"There was a retrieval failure—"

"You told me you got rid of the bugs."

"I did, sir. I don't know what happened."

"What did Trimble say when he reported it?"

"He didn't; he ran off before I could get to him."

"Sonuvabitch. Where's he now?"

"I dunno … you want me to track him—"

"No, never mind. I see him. I'll have him taken to the Doc; I wish you people would get a handle on this shit...."

"Yes, sir."

Pause.

"Kid, you know your staying in the barracks is for the good of the project?"

"I guess so...."

"Good. After Monday, everything will be back to normal. Now, you workin' on the packet?"

"Yes, sir. Should I postpone Monday's orientation until—"

"No! We'll figure it out. Everything goes as planned."

"Yes, sir."

CHAPTER 7

After Pierce clicked off, Hedges sat and stared at the wall of paper-thin displays. He was in the Ops Center, a place where he'd spent most waking hours, since finding the Grid beacon.

The large, spartan room—its curved walls plastered with the latest in display technology—used to be one of his favorite places. But now, it was just as much a prison as the studio in the barracks.

Even before the Marvin Trimble alert, Hedges was having trouble concentrating. The cotton haze in his head was caused by a combination of jetlag, neural recording fatigue, and worry over the fate of Earth's Grid access. Not to mention the stress of being locked up, like some animal ... and the system issues only compounded the problem.

After the alert, he'd gone to PIT-2—Marvin's immersion room—and examined the Onculus, but the results of his diagnostic indicated the equipment was functioning as designed.

Then, he'd run a full system scan, and again, found nothing anomalous. The Quantum Intelligence Neural Network had been remarkably stable for a new technology, so why this issue, why now? Why had it only retrieved 95% of the Cerulean immersion?

He was at a loss: just as there'd been no course at Caltech on how to deal with sociopathic bosses, there'd been nothing on troubleshooting otherworldly quantum systems. It wasn't as if he could download *Intergalactic Quantum Networks for Noobs* and skip to the troubleshooting guide.

Sure, he had the limited instructions he'd received from Uri—after he'd trapped the beacon in the collector array—but there were no references to partial packet retrievals. Which made sense; each planet designed their immersion retrieval and playback systems in slightly different ways.

Hedges tried to focus, but fighting through the cotton in his head was like hacking through a jungle with a dull machete, and his mind kept replaying Pierce's whiskey-fueled confession.

He couldn't believe there'd been a time when he'd admired the Pantheon Director ... had actually looked up to the guy.

But he wasn't alone; he'd landed the Holy Grail job in his field. It was the only thing any of his peers had ever talked about: working for Pantheon, or getting inside any one of Pierce's multinational corporations.

Hedges had been the chosen one, had won out over all others. What he hadn't signed up for, though, was being saddled with the burden of preserving Earth's tenuous connection to an alien network! Another thing not listed in the Caltech course catalog.

Now that he knew—and he was sure he was the only one who knew about Pierce's true intentions—it would be up to him to put a stop to it. But he had yet to come up with a workable plan and he was almost out of time.

He shook his head and tried to focus on the task at hand. He picked up his tablet and tapped an icon.

Computer code appeared on the center screen, the largest screen on the curved wall. The code was from the program responsible for executing transfers between the Onculus and QUINN.

After spending nearly an hour poring over the code—going over it, line-by-line—Hedges sat back, defeated. If there were errors, he couldn't see them.

He decided to give it a rest; maybe focusing on something else would help clear the cobwebs.

CHAPTER 8

Quantum physicist Oscar Rand left his house in a hurry, anxious to get to his lab. Anxious to tweak his experiment.

He steered his Prius onto Pantheon Parkway and—through the open window—he thought he smelled Halloween, even though the holiday was still weeks away.

When he picked up his coffee and sipped, he realized the scent of the spiced-pumpkin latte might have something to do with his visions of trick-or-treaters trudging along rainy sidewalks, mushing over fallen leaves, and clutching their sugary hauls in chubby fingers....

Up ahead, Oscar saw the outline of the Agrippa Research Complex, sprawled at the foot of Catoctin Mountain. The complex was one of many such research parks owned by Pantheon Holdings.

Agrippa occupied a vast swath of land near Leesburg, Virginia, thirty miles outside Washington, D.C.; it was the newest Pantheon development and the one Derrick Pierce had deemed worthy of its headquarters.

Oscar glanced at the headlines scrolling across the car's video display.

NEWS FOR SATURDAY, OCTOBER 3, 2015
WORLD LEADERS PREP FOR SUNDAY'S
SUMMIT ... play
SOCIOPATHIC PERSONALITY DISORDER: FOUR
TIMES MORE PREVALENT AMONG CEOs ... play

"Now there's a shocker," he muttered and pressed PLAY.

The video buffered and the modulated voice of a female reporter filled the car.

"A Columbia University research study revealed that, when compared with the rest of the population, there are a disproportionate number of sociopaths in the boardroom. Researchers found the incidence of sociopathy among business leaders was around 5%. Sociopathic traits, such as lack of empathy and lack of remorse or kindness, are advantageous when making business decisions. In some ways, executives on the mildly sociopathic end of the spectrum are successful *because* of those tendencies and not in spite of—"

Oscar shook his head and flipped off the video. "Crazy boss's. And that, ladies and gentleman," he said, holding up his coffee cup, as though he were giving a speech to the empty car, "is why I work alone. For peanuts, yes, but alone...."

His car approached the Agrippa security gate and he waited while the parking tag on his windshield was scanned. The gate opened smoothly.

He pulled forward and, up ahead, he could now see the buildings of Agrippa more clearly: squat, round buildings, four stories high, with alternating stripes of light and dark brick.

It might have been any cookie-cutter office park in any United States suburb, but this complex—in honor of its Texan owner—was arranged in the shape of a horseshoe. The expanse in the middle was filled with—among other things—a helipad, a putting green, a parking area for gourmet food trucks, and a health club.

The scientists who worked there—the thousands of physicists, mathematicians, biologists, neurologists, and engineers—called the entire complex *the Ranch.*

Oscar drove into an underground parking structure and maneuvered into a spot marked O. RAND, Ph.D., BUILDING P.

It was Saturday, and all was quiet at the Ranch; there were only a few other cars in the lot, including several black vans and a late-model Mercedes.

He got out of the car, then ducked back in to grab his latte. As he straightened, he was startled by a loud crash. It sounded like an exit door banging against the concrete garage wall; the sound was amplified by the emptiness of the lot.

Oscar turned and was surprised to see a door he'd never noticed before. Then, he saw a man, one who looked vaguely familiar, stumble into the garage.

The man was short, balding, and wore a rumpled suit. As he neared, Oscar recognized Pantheon's director of human resources.

It had been a while since Oscar interviewed for the Pantheon technical engineer job—back when he'd briefly considered working for the corporate overlords—and he couldn't remember the man's name.

At the last second, it came to him and he called out, "Hey, Marvin, you okay?"

Unfocused eyes skittered over Oscar and Marvin bumped into him, hard enough to cause Oscar's coffee to tip over and dribble a few drops onto his BARACK THE VOTE t-shirt.

But Marvin didn't pause, didn't acknowledge Oscar, he just stumbled farther into the garage, toward the Mercedes. He either hadn't seen Oscar or was deliberately ignoring him.

Oscar shrugged and turned, continuing on to the elevators. Everyone knew the Pantheon people were strange; besides, he had other things on his mind.

He didn't notice when Marvin was intercepted by two men in black.

CHAPTER 9

Marvin wasn't surprised to see Pantheon security and, though he may not be a genius, he knew well enough to accompany them back into the building—back underground.

They led him down the wide, brightly lit hallway, past PIT-2, where—moments before—he'd walked tall within the Cerulean landscape.

His head throbbed and he berated himself: why hadn't he just reported the issue? Nobody ignored a Derrick Pierce directive—that was rule number one—

They stopped when they'd reached Dr. Neil Thompson's office. The guards deposited Marvin in the waiting room, then left.

Filled with nervous energy, Marvin sat and flipped through a magazine, his knee bounced up and down. At one point, he looked through a small window in one of the side doors and could have sworn he saw President deGrey walk by. *My brain must really be fried,* he thought, and shook his head.

He glanced back a moment later, but saw no one.

Finally, Dr. Thompson, a neurologist in his early sixties—distinguished with salt-and-pepper hair—opened a door to the left of the waiting area.

He smiled. "Hello, Marvin; come on back."

Marvin stood and followed. He tried to keep pace, but the Doc walked in long, brisk strides, making it difficult for Marvin's short legs to keep up. Soon—too soon—they reached the implantation room.

Marvin hesitated at the threshold while Thompson stood to the side. Finally, he walked in.

"Have a seat."

He complied; the paper on the exam chair crackled as he settled in.

Thompson washed his hands, then sighed and said, "Marvin, you know any issues with the Onculus must be reported to Hedges ... immediately. Why didn't you?"

"I don't know." Marvin lowered his head, feeling like a child being admonished for not flossing.

Thompson placed a hand on his shoulder. "It's probably not that serious; we'll just scan your implant and see what's going on."

The Doc picked up something that looked like a cross between a handheld scanner and a stun gun. He pressed a button on the side and rubbed it across Marvin's forehead.

Beep!

Thompson pulled the scanner back and looked down at the digital readout.

Marvin leaned over and peeked at the message.

PIT-MTi: 0 OF 1TnBITS. FORMATTED

The readout faded and Thompson looked at Marvin, who sat up.

Crackle, crackle.

He hoped they were done; all he wanted to do was to go home and crawl in bed with Naomi.

"Sorry, but I've had to disable your implant; I'll check with Mr. Pierce, but I think that—until the system error is investigated—it's probably best you abstain from immersion travel. Perhaps, once the issues are resolved, we can reactivate your implant. Sound good?"

Marvin shrugged; he loved immersion travel but was ambivalent about getting a new implant. Was in no hurry to get another injection.

Maybe it was time for him to focus his attention on Naomi; he already felt guilty about not telling her about the Grid ... about immersions.

The Doc studied Marvin, seeming to consider something.

Marvin squirmed under the scrutiny.

Finally, Thompson stood and his chair rolled back. "Excuse me," he said and left the room.

A minute ticked by and Marvin hoped he wasn't in for one of those marathon waits—the kind he was sure they taught in first year med school. A wait so long you were convinced that they'd forgotten about you and all the doctors and nurses had closed up shop and left you sitting there on crackle paper in an assless gown—

Thankfully, no more than two minutes passed before the doctor returned.

Thompson walked to the counter next to the sink and began scribbling on a chart.

"How're you sleeping these days?" he asked.

"Not so great, I guess ... the tossing and turning is driving my fiancée nuts."

"Naomi, right? The knockout from reception?" *Scribble, scribble.* "I don't know how you pulled that off ... when's the wedding?"

Thompson lobbed a series of questions Marvin knew didn't require responses, then he said, "I'm going to give you a little something to help you sleep...."

He reached into the cabinets above the sink and returned to the chair. He held out a prescription bottle. No label.

"Take a few of these sedatives and by morning, your tired neurons will no longer be an issue."

"Thanks, Doc."

Marvin took the bottle and left.

CHAPTER 10

Neil Thompson stood at the sink, hands dripping. After a moment, he said, "There was nothing on the implant."

Silence.

I know you're there.

He dried his hands and tossed the paper towel into a bin. He leaned back against the counter and crossed his arms.

First, there was a clicking sound, then a voice filled the room.

"You're sure there's nothing there? Why the alert? Why couldn't the Onculus get the full packet from his implant? I mean, the damn stuff didn't just disappear, right?"

Thompson tilted his head, never sure where to direct his voice.

"Honestly, I couldn't say."

"So ... now what? I got a big day on Monday—"

"Sir, there's nothing more I can do ... whatever the problem, it's not the implant. Maybe check with Hedges—I'm sure boy genius will have some ideas."

He waited for a response, but soon realized the COMM feed was no longer on.

Sociopath.

To be fair, Thompson had been the one to send Marvin home with the high-dose amitriptyline—a sedative sure to induce a heart attack in a patient with Marvin's condition—but he was merely following orders.

No, *Pierce* was the sociopath—of that he was certain—and he had the Director's MRI scans to support the diagnosis.

Before implantation, all prospective PIT users were required to undergo a full neurological work-up to assess compatibility with immersion travel. When it came time to scan Pierce's brain, Thompson detected a small lesion in his ventromedial prefrontal cortex.

Several years prior, he'd observed the same lesions during a study of the neurology of sociopaths and serial killers. There, he'd spent many months comparing abnormal brain scans to normals, and the results pointed to a strong association of damage to the VMPFC and a subsequent corruption of the inherent moral network in the human brain.

Of course, not everyone with such lesions would turn out to be psycho killers—sociopathy was a spectrum disorder—but the indicators were there, in Pierce's brain.

As he observed Pierce's behavior, Thompson believed him to be on the more benign end of the spectrum, with delusions of grandeur being the most obvious manifestation, but increasingly, he wasn't so sure....

Because Pierce's neural pathways were compromised by the lesion in his VMPFC, Thompson concluded that the Director was one of a small percentage of the population not suited for implantation and immersion.

It wasn't the implantation procedure—the injection into the thalamus of the brain-computer interface—that was the problem.

In Pierce's brain, the bioelectronics microchip would be like a ticking time bomb. When he tried to play back an immersion's recorded sequence of electrical impulses, action potentials and neural firings, eventually, the sequence would encounter the lesion roadblock; if an immersion involved signaling the VMPFC in any way, the bomb could detonate.

Sometimes, the playback would skip over the lesion and signal the rest of the firing sequence, other times, the playback would be thrown into an undefined loop, eventually causing the implant to short-circuit.

If that happened, glial tissue would scar over the implant, further impairing the thalamic pathways—the conductor neurons that dispatch information about sensation and perception, telling the brain how to interpret visual and auditory signals.

Thompson explained all that to Pierce, who waved it away, accusing Thompson of being too cautious, and ordered him to perform the procedure.

A more resolute man might have stood his ground, but Thompson was aware of his own failings. And so, he performed the implantation....

And, Pierce still blamed Thompson for what happened.

He sighed, feeling as though he'd aged ten years since joining the Pantheon payroll. Pierce had charmed him into coming out of retirement, and when Thompson learned of the scope of the project—of the Grid, of the bioelectronic and nanotech applications he'd get to work with—he couldn't say no; it was the dream job for anyone with his research interests.

Somewhere along the way, as he got deeper into the project, he'd incrementally been asked to do things that danced along the edge of ethics violations. It was so pernicious, he lost sight of the edge, and—before he knew it—was well beyond. Too far, he thought, to go back.

He told himself he remained to keep an eye on Pierce, but it didn't take much soul-searching to uncover the truth. He stayed and kept quiet because he wanted to continue on with the revolutionary work.

CHAPTER 11

With coffee cup in hand, Oscar Rand stood in his lab, feeling nostalgic. Monday would kick-off his last week at the Ranch; his funding was running out and so goes the lease on his research facility.

He looked around and took a sip of the now tepid latte.

Perhaps *facility* was stretching it, but that's what he'd called it in his 2013 grant proposal: *Detecting, Trapping, and Recombining Entangled Crystal Q-Gates.* In reality, the *facility* was one small room occupying the corner of the first floor of Building P.

In contrast to the sleek, well-funded research labs throughout the Ranch, Oscar's was no more than a moderately high-tech broom closet. But, since he was the only one working there each day, pinging pre-entangled particles throughout the Universe—or trying to, anyway—the space was adequate.

His meager equipment had been cobbled together thanks to generous donors—mostly MIT alumni—people who still had faith in his theories.

Oscar walked to the long folding table which was set up underneath the window. On the table was his meager equipment: an ion trap, a q-state analyzer, and a woefully old laptop.

He called his system 'Q-bert', in honor of the video game his dad—his *real* dad—had left behind, back at the old house in Boston.

Playing the classic arcade game in the basement rec-room had made him feel close to the man he barely remembered. In fact, he wasn't sure if the few memories he had were real, or were the kind manufactured after seeing the same photo over and over.

But, after a while, he no longer had the video game as a way of feeling connected. One day, after school, Oscar had run down to the basement only to find Q-bert was gone. His step-father had replaced it with a big screen TV, a beer-filled fridge, and a ratty old recliner riddled with cigar burns.

Shaking off unpleasant memories of the past, Oscar concentrated on his *Eureka!* moment of the morning.

It had happened in the shower, the one place his mind seemed most receptive to novel ideas. Terrified he'd lose the idea, he'd cut his shower short, threw on the nearest t-shirt and jeans, and rushed to the Ranch.

He couldn't believe he hadn't thought of it before. It was just a simple reversal of his existing experiment. Instead of being the fish, he'd be the fisherman.

Instead of indiscriminately sending out particles tagged with his quantum cryptographic signature—hoping some random being in the Cosmos would notice—he would cast a net of his own, one that would sniff out the crypto signature of some *other* Oscar out there.

Those other Oscars had to be out there ... right, Frank?

He glanced over at the far wall, at the poster with Frank Drake's 1961 equation—the one that computed a hypothetical number of intelligent civilizations in a single galaxy—civilizations that might have developed the ability to send signals into deep space.

$$N = R^* \cdot f_p \cdot n_e \cdot f_l \cdot f_i \cdot f_c \cdot L$$

N being the product of several factors, including the rate of star formation each year in a single galaxy, how many stars have planets, the fraction of those planets that could support life, what fraction of those civilizations are intelligent, what fraction of those have developed the tech to send out signals, and finally, how long it would be before those civilizations released the signals into space.

In his doctoral thesis, Oscar had further modified the equation to include the fraction of civilizations with the ability to detect and affect quantum states. Still—he believed—it would be a very large *N*: a respectable number of such civilizations, just in the Milky Way alone, never mind the *N* that might exist in the rest of the galaxies....

But, Oscar's pings had never been returned.

Who knew? Maybe his pinging was already being detected throughout the Universe. Maybe he was disturbing the aliens every day, like clockwork, from 9 to 5....

"Honey, there's that PING! again. Did you hear it? Honey?"

"Yes, I heard it. For heaven's sake ... it's just the machine that goes PING! Now go back to sleep."

Oscar grinned and sat down. He opened his laptop, anxious to revise his experiment code. Anxious to start fishing.

For the past two years, he'd been collecting particles in his ion trap—tagging them with his q-signature—hoping the state change reflected on the particles' entangled twins would be noticed by someone or some*thing*.

He'd done it with trillions of particles, but so far, had elicited no response. Nothing had ever appeared in his ion trap—nothing suggesting exoplanetary origins, that is.

But this time, he would look for particles that had been manipulated by another hand, by another being, on another planet, in another galaxy.

Such manipulations of q-states should be easier to detect, because, just as he was tagging particles with his own crypto, the other Oscars would as well.

Hypothetically.

And, unintentionally, every code writer has a unique signature, a way of coding and tagging, as unique as a fingerprint. Oscar would revise an existing signature detection program to test his new hypothesis.

He opened his original experiment file. Then, he revised the Ekert quantum cryptography detection cypher.

At first, he would only scoop his own tagged ions, but if it worked, he'd have something to publish—something to bring to his investors. Then maybe, he could justify the expense of an ionospheric collector array.

Up there, in high-Earth orbit, the fish would be much more interesting....

If he was successful, he might even be able to keep his lease and remain at Agrippa for a while longer. Near his friends.

Satisfied his experiment was ready, Oscar closed his eyes, said a little prayer, and pressed RUN.

CHAPTER 12

Senator Walter Higgs stood outside Derrick Pierce's office. The Chairman of the Science, Space and Technology Committee was dressed for golf and would've been on the first tee if he hadn't been summoned to see the Great One, effectively ruining his Saturday. It was his only free day before the G-10 Summit....

If President deGrey hadn't insisted on giving him a lift,

("Don't be silly; I'm headed that way myself.")

it was unlikely he'd have agreed to come.

Where deGrey and the Secret Service agents had gone—after Marine One landed—was anyone's guess.

Whatever it was the Crazy Cowboy wanted, Walter hoped he'd get straight to the point. In truth, he had a pretty good idea what the summons was about....

Pierce probably wanted to give Walter marching orders for Geneva. Orders for deals he wanted made. Pierce—a notorious recluse—was always invited, but never went. Instead, he sent others armed with laundry lists of things he wanted done.

One thing was certain; Pierce wouldn't be interested in discussing any of the official G-10 agenda items. He wouldn't be interested in such things as world hunger, clean energy, or peaceful, political transition plans.

In that respect, Pierce wasn't much different from most Summit attendees. The official agenda, the one the media received, was window-dressing, designed to give the perception that someone, somewhere, was working on the issues.

Meanwhile, the *real* business of the world was conducted behind-the-scenes, in hushed side meetings. Meetings between bedfellows the public would never envisage.

Walter sighed and rubbed a hand over his bald head. Then, he knocked on the office door.

"Come in."

Walter entered and the first thing he noticed was the smell of cigar smoke. Then he saw the wall of windows overlooking the Agrippa Complex, overlooking the helipad where Marine One waited.

"Glad you could make it."

Upon hearing the southern drawl, Walter looked to his right.

Smoking a cigar, with his cowboy boots kicked up on a Texas-sized desk, was Derrick Pierce. The only thing missing from the scene, Walter thought, was a pair of bull horns mounted to the front of the desk.

"Derrick," he nodded toward Pierce then glanced around the office. The décor was a discordant hodgepodge of dark wood, overpriced art, and high-tech gadgetry. "Love what you've done with the place," he said, aware he sounded churlish, but he was still chafing at the summons.

But then—in the middle of the office—he spotted something that wasn't so terrible. "*This*, however, now *this* is interesting," he mused and moved toward the object.

Cradled inside a velvet-lined box, set atop a pedestal, was an old, single-action Army revolver.

"What a spectacular find," he breathed.

"Thanks," Pierce smiled, white teeth flashing against tanned skin. He stood, tugged at his shirt cuffs, and walked over to the box. He pulled the gun out and handed it to Walter.

"That there was commissioned by none other than Butch Cassidy. Most folks believe there was only one Sundance Colt, the one Butch made for the Sundance Kid, but he actually had two made … he gave one to Kit Madden and the other to Sundance. The one I have—the one you're holdin'—is the real Sundance Colt … the only one engraved with the "S"… see it right there, on the butt? Nice, ain't it?"

Walter turned the gun over and traced the "S" with his fingertip. He admired the nickel finish and mother of pearl grips. "Very nice," he admitted.

Pierce—apparently done with show and tell—took the gun and waved at a chair. "Have a seat," he said, and tossed the gun onto a stack of papers.

He leaned down, opened a drawer, and held up a bottle. "Some o' the friendly creature?"

"Huh?" Walter asked, annoyed. He was trying his best to be patient; he didn't care for Derrick Pierce, but they were tied together by virtue of aligned interests.

He had to hold his tongue. Had to refrain from telling Pierce exactly what he could do with his *friendly creature*, whatever godforsaken, backwater thing that was.

"Whiskey?" Pierce smiled and again reached down, this time coming up with two crystal glasses.

Walter, his irritation exacerbated by Pierce's good-ol'-boy act, thought, *Just say "whiskey" then, and spare me the cornpone....*

It had been a long time since Pierce had set foot in Texas, since he'd worked in his father's oilfields. But that wasn't the only reason the drawl rankled. Everybody who had regular dealings with Pierce knew the extra layer of down home signaled one of two things: either he was out to charm you, or to destroy you.

Walter had been on the receiving end of both and just wanted to know what was on the day's menu. He shrugged and said, "Sure ... fine. Now, can you please tell me why I gave up eighteen at Augusta?"

"Relax, Wally; geez, you Yankees are so impatient." Pierce handed a glass to Walter. "You goin' to Geneva tomorrow?"

So there it was—Pierce *did* want to discuss the Summit.

Walter sipped the whiskey and wondered what his Majesty wanted this go-round. Last year, he wanted piggyback contracts for all future satellite launches. Anything in high-Earth orbit, GPS or spy-sats, no matter. And, Pierce didn't care whose they were—Russian, German, Chinese—Walter had been instructed to get them all.

He'd obliged. He played errand boy and got it done, never knowing what payload Pierce was sending up.

That was last year.

This year, Walter had plans of his own and his meeting dance card was nearly full, with one meeting in particular destined to solidify the Senator as a major player. His plans didn't include Pierce. Whatever Pierce wanted, it would have to take a back seat.

"Yes, I'll be there," Walter replied and steeled himself for the pitch....

But, as it turned out, Pierce wasn't interested in Geneva.

The Pantheon director sat with his hands tented in front of his mouth, barely concealing a smile, and Walter realized then that Pierce was about to burst, like he had a secret he couldn't wait to share.

"The reason I called you here today was to tell you about a recent discovery of mine: a quantum networking device, capable of receiving and sending high-volume data—instantaneously—across the Universe. A device that has discovered an alien internet," Pierce lobbed the statement into the air like a grenade and paused, as though waiting for the Senator to jump on it.

He'd be waiting a while, Walter thought. He wasn't sure whether to laugh or feel insulted. In the end, he responded in kind.

"And I shall now turn into a goat and fly 'round this office whilst spinning assholes out of angel wings."

CHAPTER 13

Oscar stared at the ion trap's LED screen. If his revised experiment worked, any particles snagged with his crypto would be trapped and a laser would extract the data.

His pulse quickened when—toward the end of the program's run—there was a flicker on the screen. He glanced at the laptop, at the program output frame, hoping there'd be something there.

But there wasn't.

Nevertheless, Oscar was encouraged by the flicker. He reset everything and reran the program.

He stepped back and waited, his arms crossed, and gnawed on a thumbnail. Then he saw a similar flicker in the ion trap, followed by another, then another, until a shape formed in the trap—a crystal—and something appeared in the output file.

Something! Did he finally have results?! After all this time?

Oscar's head began to buzz, and he tried to temper his enthusiasm—to remind himself any result could be due to a coding error or random bug. He told himself his desire for results was probably heightened by virtue of being so close to his grant's expiration....

He scrolled through the program error log and saw nothing anomalous, then, he perused the output.

His system had recaptured 100% of the ions with his signature! The crypto detection program had correctly snagged particles with his signature, just as he'd hoped.

As Oscar scrolled through the output, he realized there was something else—particles with a different signature.

That can't be right.

He wondered if there was an error in his detection algorithm, perhaps, something that allowed non-tagged particulates through the sieve.

He sat at the laptop and examined the extracted quanta, the data that wasn't tagged with his crypto. As he scrolled through the code, his excitement became difficult to reign in.

The code wasn't in any format or syntax he recognized, and he was at least somewhat familiar with all known programming languages, most he knew backward and forward.

But this code was foreign.

A good sign, Oscar thought, a very good sign; the more unidentifiable the output, the better.

He tried everything in his arsenal—used every known decryption program and algorithm—but to no avail, and each time a method failed, the more optimistic he became.

Could he really *be looking at exoplanetary quanta?!*

His mind was off to the races then; he couldn't stop it. He couldn't remember the last time he was faced with code he couldn't understand—at least on some basic level—

Then, Oscar saw something that brought his mind back to a canter; his heart sank and his pulse returned to normal.

Crap on a cracker.

There, among the foreign code and odd syntax, were regular, boring, English words ... human words: neuromap, electrical impulse, synapse, central nervous system, caudate nucleus. Then, a few words not like the others: Cerulean and QUINN.

Whatever the data was, wherever it was from, it appeared to be related to neurology.

Oscar stared at the output for a while, then grabbed his coffee. He sipped, grimaced, and set it back on the desk. *Cold.*

He'd been nursing the coffee all morning, aware that seven-dollar lattes would soon be a luxury he couldn't afford; the closer he got to the end of his grant, the more frugal he had to be. The last thing he wanted was to go crawling back home.

He shuddered at the thought of moving back in with his mom and, God forbid, his stepfather. He'd work for the corporate overlords before he did *that....*

Oscar stood and paced and—every so often—glanced at the ion trap, then at the laptop. He supposed he should be grateful for *any* result, even if it appeared to be data grabbed from his own planet.

Had he glommed onto a particle from some other physicist's lab, in one of the other buildings at the Ranch? Or, maybe it was from another state, or another country. Either way, it was more than he'd ever trapped.

With the variety of research projects going on at any given time at Agrippa, it wouldn't be farfetched to consider someone else was affecting quanta.

Hoping to validate his results, Oscar reset everything and ran the experiment again. He removed the reference to his signature, hoping the program would only capture the unknown crypto.

This time, however, there were no flashes and nothing appeared in the ion trap.

He tried a dozen more times.

Still nothing.

He sat and stared at the first set of output results and warmed to the notion that he might have crossed particles with some other scientist's experiment at the Ranch—he knew of at least three other physicists that—

Of course!

Oscar grabbed his cell phone, shaking his head, amazed Teddy Lawson hadn't come to mind the moment he'd seen the neuro jibber-jabber.

"Hey, numbnuts, what's up?" Teddy asked, before Oscar had a chance to say hello. "No, wait ... don't tell me ... you're at the Ranch?"

"As a matter of fact—"

"Oh, man, you gotta get a life. Particles can't keep you warm at night, my friend."

Oscar smiled. "Well, actually, they can...."

He heard music in the background; Teddy was, no doubt, playing pool. It was the weekend after all, and that's what normal people did. They went out in the world and mixed in with the rest of society.

He and Teddy had met at MIT, in a class on neuroinformatics and nanomaterials. Along the way, they discovered a mutual love of *Dr. Who* and *Monte Python* and became fast friends.

"Anyway, I think I may have found something," Oscar said, trying to get Teddy to focus.

The sounds on the other end were muffled and he heard: "You call that a break?" Then, Teddy spoke directly into the phone. "So, what did ya find?"

"Can you come to the lab? It'd probably be easiest to just show you—"

"Aw man, you know I hate to be there on the weekend...."

Teddy worked at Neuropath Labs, in Building T. A good thing, too; if it weren't for his friend dragging him to the food trucks every so often, he'd never eat lunch; he got so wrapped up in his work, things like food and life were all but forgotten.

"Come on," Oscar pleaded. "I'll let you beat me at pool."

He was pretty certain he could ask Teddy for anything—*almost* anything—but there was a dance to be done and bribes to be made....

"Fine, I'll be there ... but the beers are on you."

Oscar smiled, hung up, and looked back at his laptop. If anyone could help him translate this mystery data, it would be Teddy.

CHAPTER 14

"Hey, numbnuts!" Teddy's greeting was loud enough to carry from the elevators all the way down the hall, through the open lab door.

"Hey, jerkytits!" Oscar responded and his heart skipped.

Then, he remembered his rushed departure from the house and knew his hair was sticking out all over the place. It was naturally a hopeless puffball, but, when he had time—when he wasn't having an *aha!* moment—he usually managed to get it under some semblance of control.

He looked down and noticed the coffee stain on his t-shirt, just under Obama's pearly whites. Oh, well, he thought. There wasn't much he could do about his appearance—

Teddy bounded through the doorway with a lopsided grin on her face. She was a petite brunette, with dimples and freckles and—Oscar noticed—a blue smudge on her cheek.

She has no idea how damn cute she is, Oscar thought, and for a moment, he forgot all about aliens and entangled particles.

Theodora *'Don'tyoudarecallmethat'* Lawson, Ph.D., was twenty-seven—two years older than Oscar. She wore a loose-fitting, camouflage-print tank top and black pants. And, Oscar could see— peeking out from underneath her top—the ribbons of a pink corset.

Christ, he thought, *those corsets will be the end of me.*

He felt his face flush and he tore his eyes away from the ribbons.

He didn't think Teddy realized people could see hints of the corsets—some lace here and a ribbon there—underneath her tomboy clothes. Or maybe he was the only one looking that close? All he knew was, outside of the Civil War reenactments he drug her to, she wouldn't be caught dead in frilly things.

"How's the wonderful world of the insignificant?" She asked.

Oscar smiled. "The very small, you mean?"

"Right," she smiled up at him and shrugged. Then, she noticed he was staring at her. "Whataya lookin' at?"

"You've got something on your face." Before he could stop himself, Oscar reached out and swiped a finger across her flushed cheek. He turned his finger over and showed her the blue chalk.

"Very cute," he said, trying to make it sound light and playful. Instead, the words came out hoarse and crackly.

Thankfully, she didn't seem to notice the effect she had on him.

"Such a dork," she smiled and pushed his hand away. She walked over to the desk and flopped into a chair. "So what am I doing here? You know I love ya, but I've got a live one back at *Rooney's*."

Yeah ... focus, LoverBoy.

Oscar pulled his mind back to the business at hand, to the unusual data he'd found.

"Right, sorry about that. Q-bert seems to have found something—I don't know what—but whatever it is, it looks like a bunch of neuro-speak. Hence, milady," he said, and did a partial bow, "the need for your expertise."

Teddy perked up at the mention of neurology. "Found? How so?"

Oscar sat down next to her and talked her through his experiment, step-by-step, explaining the coding tweaks he'd made. It wasn't long before she was giving him that look, the one that said: "Quit talking to me like I'm a noob".

She smiled and raised an eyebrow. "I got it, Belabor Bob. You were doing your 'let's call up E.T.' thing and you finally got a response, only, the party on the other end was local, not long-distance like you'd hoped."

"Exactly," he nodded, relieved. He pushed the laptop toward her. "Take a look and see what you think."

Teddy scrolled through the program output, then said, "Based on the plain-text and syntax, it looks like bioinformatics stuff, some brain-computer interface program, maybe. Interneurons, functional sensory integration, action potentials, cortical firing rate, optic tract, thalamus, input stimulus, electrical impulses, visuospatial interpolation, cortical loci ... yeah ... definitely bioinformatics or BCI. Definitely."

"OK, Rain Man," Oscar teased. Then, he was distracted by the remnants of blue chalk on her cheek. With effort, he resisted the urge to touch her smooth skin. "But, a program for what? A virtual reality game ... brain surgery?"

"I don't know," she shook her head. "We could load the code into my brainmap software. Maybe recreate part of the original program."

"Let's try it."

Teddy signed into her cloud storage and opened a program called N-MAP. She started a new project, pasted in the code from Oscar's experiment results, and pressed RUN.

They waited as the program crunched and, when it was done, something unusual appeared in the results window.

"Whoa," they said in unison and bolted upright.

CHAPTER 15

Crisp images of an otherworldly landscape appeared. Oscar peered at the images, his nose inches from the screen, and mumbled, "What the heck *is* that?"

Teddy shook her head and shrugged. "Not sure, although, I think I may have worked on code like this...."

She scrolled through several more pages of the code, then continued. "A few months ago, Neuropath lent me out to consult on one of those puzzle projects; you know, where a bunch of contractors get a different piece, none ever seeing the final picture. Usually it's classified stuff, so I didn't ask questions. I mean, the pay was insane, so who cares, right? Anyway, this syntax is similar to the code my team worked on."

"Can you tell by the code what the program is supposed to do? Is it a game?"

"I don't know. With so little to go on," Teddy said, flipping back and forth between the image fragments and the code, "it's still just part of a larger puzzle—wait a minute...." She zoomed in on one of the images. "Does that look like a logo to you?"

Oscar studied the image. "Maybe. Could be...."

The partial image looked like a badge icon, about two inches in diameter, dark blue with gold trim. The letters E-O-N were visible in the lower right portion of the circle.

"I know that logo! We should have recognized it right away," Oscar looked up and pointed out the window, at the signage in front of the building next door.

Pantheon's familiar badge logo was a perfect match.

CHAPTER 16

Oscar was uneasy. "So ... it's Pantheon stuff?"

His excitement waned; the heady notion he'd finally have results to show his investors—something to publish—was overshadowed by something else. Something ominous.

The last time someone hacked Pantheon—and what Oscar had done could be defined as such—the hacker disappeared. Leaving no trace she'd ever existed. At least, that was the gist of that particular urban legend, one of many Pantheon-related myths.

Rumors abounded at the Ranch about the world-dominating conglomerate: rumors about its projects, about its military intelligence affiliations, and about its eccentric director, Derrick Pierce.

This was different from snagging data from a nearby lab, from some friendly neurogeek in a public research facility. Pantheon, along with developing some of the world's most advanced personal tech, was also the government's primary intelligence contractor.

And here he sat, looking at data his ion trap had innocently snagged, with a crypto signature that had apparently been scripted to particles—by someone at Pantheon.

It was discomfiting.

But soon, Oscar's scientific curiosity overrode his apprehension, and he wondered what sort of quantum detection equipment a billionaire might have. An ionospheric collector, surely. Perhaps an entire array....

Pantheon already had a blanket of satellites in high-Earth orbit; it wouldn't take much for them to put together a monster collector array—

He was startled from his thoughts when Teddy suddenly shouted, "Recognition software!"

She opened another program, pasted in the images Oscar had found, and started a comparison search.

They watched as the partial fragments were compared with millions of images from thousands of databases throughout the world—commercial, government, academic—but, when the comparison was complete, no match had been found.

Whatever program the fragments belonged to, it didn't appear to have been published.

"Damn," Oscar slumped back in his chair. "Well, it was a good idea, anyway."

He and Teddy sat and stared at the images, at the otherworldly landscapes and the badge logo. He wondered what they were working on over at Pantheon that involved tagging ions with cryptography and again, he wondered what equipment they were using.

He also wondered why he hadn't been able to replicate his results. Had Q-bert been fishing at the right place, at precisely the right time, or was there another explanation?

Teddy finally spoke, "Do you know anyone at Pantheon? You could ask them about the file. Maybe figure out where they stored it? That might help you tweak your experiment in order to replicate your results, right?"

Oscar nodded slowly, thinking of Marvin, the HR guy. Maybe on Monday, he'd drop by Pantheon and ask—what, exactly? He wasn't sure, but he'd think of something; he was too curious to be spooked by the mythos of the place.

He'd never been in the Pantheon building; he couldn't think of a single Ranch scientist who had. Contractors like Teddy suspected they worked on Pantheon projects, but never knew for certain and never performed the work in Building Q.

As for Oscar, his interview with Marvin had been in a conference room in another building.

At any rate, on Monday—if Oscar *did* decide to go over there—he hoped the guy would be friendlier than he'd been in the parking garage....

"Yeah, I think there might be someone I could ask. But, you know those people can be pretty secretive ... I doubt they'll be thrilled with me getting hold of their data."

Teddy stood and—with a mischievous grin—hooked her arm through his. "Come on. You'd better buy me that beer before you disappear into the clutches of the evil empire."

Oscar laughed.

CHAPTER 17

[TRANSLATION: GS15-CIRCINI-Ω >>EARTH-G-α5B-3215]
In a nearby galaxy, a semi-homologous mind was occupied with thoughts of Earth—one of the newest Grid members.

Uri, Senior Technician for Grid Sector 15, stared at the blue and green orb suspended in the center of the mushroom-shaped room. He hovered alongside it, bobbling up and down.

Veldk, the long-suffering and overworked GS15 librarian, glided into the room. His tentacles bristled when he saw the towering stack of new planet carts. "How many *now*?"

"Five million."

"It's getting to be too much."

Uri bobbled in agreement; it wasn't news to him. The backlog situation had been growing ever unwieldy as their sector expanded. Beacons were being answered at an alarming rate; faster than the response algorithms had predicted.

Veldk crooked a tentacle at the planet model in the middle of the room, the one Uri had been contemplating. "Looks kinda like *our* planet," he said and reached for a blank cart. "What's its native designation?"

"Earth."

"One moon?"

Uri bobbled.

"How old?"

"Right around a+5B."

"Respectable; could have some good tech; when did the beacon response come in?"

"a5B215."

"The only one?"

"No, there were three thousand over 215."

"[Undefined expletive]; so then, EARTH-G-a5B-3215?" Veldk asked.

Uri bobbled and Veldk made a notation on the cart. "Do we have their packet?"

"Not yet; they still have time."

"They can't get full access until they share—"

"I know; they're locked out of the T-LIB, but they've been accessing immersions—as they should. It's strange, though; they haven't logged many trips ... only a fraction of their reported population."

"You know what that usually signifies...." Veldk said, with one tentacle crooked downward.

Uri bobbled, also looking concerned.

"Better look into it before the Gridmaster reviews the reports; you should be prepared." With that, Veldk glided out of the room and Uri turned back to the planet model.

Back when they'd intercepted Earth's beacon response, Uri had been thrilled. Granted, he was always pleased with new discoveries, but this one was different.

Spectral analysis revealed that Earth and his own planet, Circini-Omega, shared an identical chemical composition, right down to where it mattered: the trace elements.

When Uri showed the analyses to the rest of his GS15 colleagues, they agreed that Earth must be one of their long-lost orphan sisters—one of several planets jettisoned away from Circini-Omega's galaxy during an intergalactic collision. Now, Earth had a new orbit within a different galaxy, one its inhabitants had designated the "Milky Way".

The similarities of mineral composition and the nearly identical radiometric age were too great for Uri to ignore. That evidence—coupled with the simulated collision model—led Uri to believe theirs were—indeed—planets of the same litter, now residing in neighboring galaxies 13 million light-years apart.

Later, during the live link with Earth's representative—the one who'd responded to the Grid beacon—Uri had felt an instant connection. It may have been all in his head, a preconditioned notion that he *should* feel a kinship, but he didn't think that was so.

Now, he couldn't wait to receive their immersion packet. On Earth, humans experienced visceral sensations tied to the adrenal gland—vestigial in the beings of Circini-Omega—and Uri was looking forward to a shot of adrenaline.

CHAPTER 18

Trey Hedges was in Edit Bay-I—a mini version of the Ops Center—working on Earth's immersion packet.

With some effort, he'd been able to push the Marvin Trimble alert out of his mind. Now, he concentrated on splicing together all the scenes his neural implant had recorded over the past few weeks.

He sat back and looked at the patchwork of displays on the curved wall. Each screen was filled with a still shot of one of the scenes extracted from his implant.

Now that it was done, Hedges had to admit the recording trip had been a success. Maybe too successful. There was more footage than could fit into standard immersion packet-length and he was having a hard time deciding what to cut.

The global poll Pantheon had conducted, the one asking for opinions on Earth's best features— the must-see attractions of the world—had been done for the sole purpose of designing the recording itinerary that Pierce and Hedges had followed.

Even though nobody knew the real reason for the poll, Hedges had been under the impression they'd eventually be told about the Grid. But now, he knew that wouldn't happen. Not unless he could come up with a way to stop Pierce....

Plodding forward with the edits, he looked at the first screenshot on the left. There he was, sitting in front of a Paris café, grinning like a fool, about to take a bite of a fresh-from-the-oven croissant.

Just looking at the image was enough to light up the pleasure center of his brain in a cacophony of dopamine neurotransmission spikes, just as it had during recording. Just as it will when Grid users download and play Earth's immersion—a dopamine spike to rival those of a brain on heroin. That's how good that damn croissant had been.

Hedges didn't need to replay the scene in order to recall the scent of the warm butter melting into the pockets of flaky, doughy, golden goodness. That morning in Paris, the croissant had been the perfect accompaniment to an equally perfect café au lait.

He pressed play and watched while immersion-Hedges smiled and took that first heavenly bite. The breeze from the Seine passed by, ruffled his hair, and continued on.

The entire scene had been carefully constructed to prime his brain for optimal neural firing. And it had worked like a charm.

According to Uri, food porn scenes like that were—far and away—the most popular on the

Grid. More popular than sex. Hedges realized then that he couldn't cut Paris, not a single frame—it was too good.

But, he had to find something to cut; immersions could only run for an hour. Any longer and sensory fatigue would set in; the non-native neural firings would strain the interneuronal junction in the thalamus and could overload the carbon-based, bioelectronic microchip.

So, he moved on. He moved on to the scene he *wished* he could cut. The bungee scene.

He made quick work of editing the scene, not wanting to spend any more time on it than necessary. As he added FEAR to the menu, he wondered why anyone would make the conscious decision to be afraid. There were many more sensations, pleasurable ones that still involved adrenaline—if that was their drug of choice.

He shrugged and moved on: to each his own.

The final scene was one of his favorites: the Autobahn scene.

Now, *there* was a worthy use of adrenaline. The screenshot was representative of what he'd seen through the windshield of the Lotus Elite ... what he'd been able to see, anyway; things got blurry at 190 mph. But still, that was the most fun he'd ever had.

If he were an alien looking for adrenaline, he'd choose *that* option from the Viscera menu.

Hedges wondered how much it had cost to shut down the sixty-mile stretch between

Hamburg and Berlin. Maybe the chancellor of Germany owed Pierce a favor. Very likely; most everyone in power did....

He decided to leave the rest of the edits for Monday, when he would convert the electrical impulses and neural firing sequences to *n*bits and qubits and feed the whole thing to QUINN.

His cotton head was returning, as were his concerns about Monday....

By then, it may all be over, one way or the other. After the immersion was approved, the tech library would be unlocked, and Pierce would finally have what he wanted.

What could he do to stop Pierce from hoarding the tech—the billions of years of innovation that had been amassed by the Grid planets? How could Pierce believe that one man on Earth should control such a thing?

The Grid had a strict policy of open sharing of information and knowledge. It would only be a matter of time before the Gridmaster realized what was going on. Only a matter of time before they discovered Earth's users were being denied access.

Then, Earth would be cut off. Before the rest of the world even knew it existed.

How could Hedges transfer evidence to the outside, without sounding like just another conspiracy loon?

He'd been toying with several ideas, but so far, nothing seemed plausible. Pierce was always underfoot, and his hovering had escalated.

Now that they were so close to the submission deadline, the Director was constantly asking about the immersion packet: "*Done with our packet? Where's the packet? Hey kid, work on the packet!*"

"Got your packet right here, Derrick," Hedges muttered, and closed out of the edit program.

"Talkin' to yerself, kid?"

CHAPTER 19

Hedges's back stiffened and his stomach twisted into knots. He hated those voice-over attacks, and now, knowing what he knew, they seemed more hostile than before.

He glanced at the COMM monitor to his left and saw the dreaded COMM: DPIERCE splayed across the screen.

He felt—at once—anger and guilt, as if Pierce could read his mind through the COMM system, as if he could hear his thoughts about leaking Pantheon info....

But Pierce sounded amused. "Be careful with shit like that or they'll send you down to the basement like a crazy aunt."

"Aren't I already here?" Hedges said, trying to make light of the situation, but then he realized it was how he felt; with the exception of their recording trip, it seemed like he'd been cooped up underground for years.

He sat back and rubbed his eyes. How long had it been since he'd had a good night's sleep? How long had it been since he'd seen someone his own age?

Silence filled the Ops Center and Hedges wondered if Pierce had switched off the feed.

Tentative, hoping there would be no response, he asked, "What can I do for you, sir?"

"Did you find out what caused the Trimble issue?"

Hedges hadn't, but he knew if he admitted to not knowing what was going on with QUINN, of not knowing the origin of the system alert, his life would become even more intolerable.

It wasn't in his nature to do shoddy work or to let things slip through the cracks, but he knew that—in his current state of mind—it was unlikely he'd find the cause of the alert. He'd done as much as he could.

So he lied. It was the first time he'd lied to his boss.

But Pierce had been lying to Hedges for months, so, *tit for tat, old man....*

"It was just a bug ... as you suspected; a minor error in the code. All fixed now."

"Ya sure? The system's secure? You better be damn sure; I don't have to tell you how important Monday is—"

"Yes, I'm sure."

"Good. Now ... I got a new password for that steel trap of yours."

Pierce rattled off a long string of letters and numbers and Hedges committed them to memory. He wondered again why the Director insisted on using passwords.

Who's gonna hack Pantheon ... God?

CHAPTER 20

Pierce sat back, puffed on his cigar, and thought of his meeting with Walter Higgs. The Senator would be a fine addition to his user roster.

It had taken some doin' to convince ol' Wally, but after a quick trip to the underground, he couldn't sign up fast enough.

Pierce liked the pitch meetings; it was fun to show the Yankee snobs what a kid from the Texas oilfields could rustle up. Now, they would have to give him the respect he deserved....

Oh sure, they pretended to respect him—when they wanted something. And they *always* wanted something. But—slithering underneath their patronizing smiles—was the implication that his dusty oil money shouldn't mix in with their ivy-scented bills, no matter the heinous things their money was put to.

If they couldn't fully appreciate his vision—the gift he had of seeing the Next Big Thing before everyone else—well, there wasn't much he could do about that.

Of course, he'd give the kid—and maybe Doc Thompson—their due, but in the end, the Grid was really *his* discovery.

Pierce looked out at the Agrippa Complex. The sun was beginning to set and the windows of the buildings reflected the fall colors. And, here and there, a window frame would catch the sun in such a way it made the crop of buildings twinkle like fireflies in a field.

Within those buildings, he'd assembled the best brain trust in history. Over the years, they seemed to follow Pierce—and his money—everywhere. Once he'd learned that genius moved in flocks, like geese in some spooky migration, it had been easy to predict.

In the '60s and '70s, the top physicists, mathematicians, and engineers settled down at NASA's Mission Control. In the '80s and '90s, they flew off to Silicon Valley and after *that* bubble burst, the flock headed toward Wall Street. By the time the markets gave up the ghost in '14, the brain trust had taken flight.

Pierce paid attention to the shifting winds and always knew when it was time to move on—just before the bird shit hit the fan. And now, his flock had settled down at Agrippa where they were more than welcome ... welcome to lay their golden eggs to their hearts' content.

He smiled, chomped down on his cigar, and picked up his tablet. He tapped on the ACCOUNTS icon and verified that Wally's user fee had been received. Then, he created a file for his newest acquisition.

Once that was done, Pierce tapped on the Grid user interface and stared at the file directory, stared at the grayed out file with the padlock icon. The contents of that file would be unlocked in less than two days.

Ever since they'd found the beacon, ever since the alien nerdlet had hinted at what the tech library contained, it was all he could think about—

Pierce's thoughts were interrupted when the COMM system clicked on, and COMM: THOMPSON appeared onscreen.

CHAPTER 21

"Sir?"

"Doc ... why aren't you with the Senator?"

"He's in the implantation room."

Pause.

"*And?*"

"He's not a good candidate."

"Whatdya mean?"

"You know there's a small fraction of the population whose neurology isn't suited for PIT travel?"

"So?"

"Senator Higgs's MRI shows a lesion in his hippocampus, and his performance on the virtual immersion test confirmed problems with topographical disorientation in novel environments."

"In English, for chrissake—"

"I can't give him an implant."

"Like hell you can't. I just showed him everything."

"Sir, this is precisely why I need to do a full work-up before you show them—"

"Yeah, yeah ... will he be able to do immersions, or what?"

"Maybe a few, then—"

"Do it! We can't turn him loose now."

"I just don't think I can … why don't we wait for a few days while I do a proper brain map—"

"No! It's gotta be today. Get it done."

Pause.

"Yes, sir."

CHAPTER 22

That evening, Marvin Trimble was happy the roller-coaster day was behind him. From the exhilaration of walking tall on Cerulean, to the fear at triggering the QUINN alert, and finally, to being hauled to Doc Thompson's office, he was exhausted.

But now, he was in the one place on Earth he was truly happy—in bed with Naomi. He looked over at his fiancée, stretched out beside him.

Naomi tossed her magazine aside. She looked up at him and smiled, causing his weak, broken-down heart to contract. She was concerned about him, he knew, and he felt guilty about his deception.

From the moment he'd laid eyes on her and saw her smiling up at him from behind the Pantheon reception desk, he'd been a goner. Which wasn't surprising; everyone who saw Naomi fell under her spell. She was a feline masterpiece: long red hair, hypnotic curves, and almond-shaped eyes.

So, that he'd fallen for her wasn't the surprising part, the surprise came when she'd said "Yes" ... to *him*.

Not that he was a troll, exactly; there'd been a time when he could have been rated a solid seven on the hotness scale; but inevitably, the hair rolled off and the paunch rolled on....

All he knew was, he'd give Naomi the world, if he could—the Universe and it killed him that he wasn't able to share with her the one thing that gave him almost as much pleasure as she did: planet immersion travel. It was unfair that she toiled in the same building where, underground each day, a privileged few got to experience the wonders of the Cosmos.

Pierce had assured him that, once the beta test was over, the discovery of the Grid would be shared with the rest of the world and Marvin hoped it would be soon. He was nearly at the end of his days and he wanted Naomi to experience it before he was gone.

She looked at him, the concern evident in her clear, green eyes. He leaned over, kissed her, and tried to reassure her. "It's okay; Doc Thompson gave me these and said that—by morning—I'd be good as new."

He held out his hand, showed her the pills, and popped them in his mouth. Then, he wrapped his arms around her and pulled her close.

As Marvin drifted off, he dreamt of wandering the Cerulean landscape. Shoulder-to-shoulder with Naomi.

CHAPTER 23

It was Monday morning and Derrick Pierce was feeling fine.

He was in the elevator, headed down to see the kid, to make sure everything was on schedule. To make sure their packet would be uploaded without a hitch.

It was his big day—Tech Day. Finally, the most important thing the Grid had to offer would be his....

As the elevator zoomed along, he imagined the treasure trove of blueprints and instruction manuals, like the precious few the alien nerdlet had doled out: like the ones they'd used to build the Onculus and the implants. But those had just been a tease, and Pierce was hooked. He wanted more.

Upon arriving at the PIT level, he exited the elevator and, as he made his way down the wide hallway, he looked at the red lights over the PIT room doors. He glanced down each corridor, and, all along the way, he saw the majority of lights were lit: immersion travel was popular.

Feeling fine.

At first, after Hedges had told him about the beacon, about the Grid, Pierce had wanted to keep the discovery to himself—it wasn't as if he needed the money. But, one afternoon, he'd been struck by another idea, and so the PIT rooms had been installed, and he'd invited a chosen few to join his beta test.

But, there would be no more invitations.

He walked past Doc Thompson's office and thought of Senator Higgs and Marvin Trimble. Wally was taken care of—fully implanted and ready for travel. As for Marvin, well, what's done is done; ya can't get to the oil without shreddin' some drills.

The HR director—not exactly user material in the first place—had been an unintended addition to his list. Marvin had wandered in on one of his discussions with Doc Thompson, a discussion about the Grid, and, to keep ol' Marv from blabbing, Pierce had no choice but to read him in.

So, on Saturday, when the Doc told him he had to dissolve Marvin's implant, it wasn't much of a loss. Doc also let it slip that the guy had a heart condition—only a few months to live—so it seemed an easy decision.

Marvin was better off anyway. He'd gone the way most people wished they could: peaceful, in his sleep. Pierce saw no other way.

An ex-user, one who'd had a taste of immersion travel but who could no longer enjoy it? Such a man might be resentful, might start runnin' his mouth about what was under Pantheon headquarters....

As he neared the Ops Center, Pierce tugged at his shirt cuffs and glanced in, ready to give Hedges final instructions, but the room was empty.

The kid wasn't in his usual spot, wasn't sitting and gawking at the wall of screens, but, he couldn't have gone far.

Hedges had been acting strangely ever since they returned from the recording trip—had taken to talkin' to himself. Was jumpy and scatterbrained. Not a good thing for a genius, not when Pierce needed the kid to be shootin' from both barrels.

So where the hell was he?

But then Pierce saw, at the end of the hall, Sheikh Kamal—Qatar's Minister of Defense—and he remembered that, not only was it tech day, it was also orientation day. The kid was probably in the auditorium, setting up.

Pierce changed direction and headed to the auditorium entrance. The double doors slid open and when he stepped inside, he saw that the Sheikh had joined the rest of the early arrivals— most of them world leaders and foreign dignitaries only just back from the G-10 Summit.

They were gathered around a long table filled with donuts, coffee, and trays of cut fruit. If he hadn't known better, he might have thought they were waiting for another boring G-10 keynote speech to begin.

But that circle-jerk was over—had wrapped up the night before—and what they were about to see and hear was more important than any rehash of the same old twaddle they might've discussed over the weekend. Pierce was sure the Grid tech would include silver bullets to tackle every problem those economic superpowers had been jawin' about.

The timing of the Summit had been a blessing *and* a curse; it didn't give him much breathing room before the deadline. But, he'd get it all done. He always did.

Remembering his reason for being in the auditorium, he looked toward the stage. Sure enough, there the kid was, fiddling with an Onculus, prepping it for demonstration.

Pierce called out, "Can I see you in the Ops Center? It'll only take a minute...."

Hedges glanced up and Pierce was struck by how tired he looked ... much older than any twenty-five-year-old had a right to look.

"Jeez, kid, yer lookin' wore out. Might get yerself a vacation, after all this."

CHAPTER 24

Hedges might have laughed at the absurdity of the comment, given that Pierce was the reason he looked and felt the way he did. But he didn't have the energy for that, besides, he was afraid any sound he made would come out like loony-bin-grade laughter. And that was no good; he couldn't save the Grid from a padded cell.

So, he didn't laugh. Instead, he followed Pierce out of the auditorium.

On the way back to the Ops Center, he thought he heard Pierce mutter, "Damn, it's Branson Ross."

But Hedges must have heard wrong. What would *Branson Ross* be doing at Pantheon?

It was well-known that the two moguls despised each other; Branson coming to Pantheon would be like God going down for high tea with the Devil.

But sure enough, when Hedges looked up, he saw Pierce's nemesis heading toward them.

When Branson drew near, Pierce stopped and tugged at his shirt cuffs. Through tight lips, he muttered, "Branson."

Hedges watched and thought how odd it was to see the Pantheon Director looking subordinate for a change. Pierce stood in front of Branson with his head lowered and his shoulders tense. He looked defiant, on the defensive.

"Derrick," Branson responded with barely concealed disdain, then he turned and smiled at Hedges.

"Trey, good to see you, how've you been? I trust this old cracker's treating you well? If not, you know there's always a place for you at JetLaunch, or WorldWater ... anywhere you'd like—just say the word."

"Thanks, Mr. Ross. It's great to see you, too." Hedges was always happy to see Branson, but was still curious why he was at Pantheon. Surely he hadn't joined the dark side....

There wasn't a day that went by when Hedges didn't regret turning down Branson's job offer. During his post-grad work, he'd interned at WorldWater, a place where he'd felt a sense of community and purpose.

But Pierce, who liked to poach talent—particularly when it was talent from one of Branson's companies—had dangled the carrot of quantum information systems and an ionospheric collector array. He had a knack for finding out exactly what top recruits wanted and made sure nobody else could offer better.

The mystery of why Branson was there was solved when Pierce said, "I'm glad you wised up and decided to join my beta test. Now quit tryin' to steal my employees and get into orientation ... trust me, you won't wanna miss it."

With that, Pierce grabbed Hedges's arm and dragged him away from Branson and into the Ops Center.

Once inside, Hedges glanced at the displays. He checked the PIT user schedule to see if any packets needed to be loaded. There was nothing waiting in the queue; for the moment, everyone was in their PIT room with their immersions underway.

The rest of the displays were trained on locations throughout the building, including the front entrance and the elevator bays, but—because of the number of high-profile people gathered in one location—most were trained on the auditorium.

It was overkill, Hedges thought; Pantheon was the most secure building in the world. Probably the safest place for any of them to be. Safer than a bomb shelter.

From the video feed, Hedges could see the VIPs were milling around, laughing, chatting, drinking coffee, and chomping on crullers.

Finally, Hedges turned and looked at Pierce. His mercurial boss seemed in high spirits and was wearing his favorite suit and lucky cowboy boots. Hedges flashed on the image of those same boots half-covering red footprints....

Pierce sat at the desk. "You got my new password tucked away in that idiotic memory of yours?"

"Eidetic."

"Right."

Hedges stifled a sigh, nodded, and sat down.

"You heard about Marvin Trimble?" Pierce asked, his hooded gaze trained on Hedges.

"Yeah. You don't think it had anything to do with QUINN, do you? Something to do with his immersion?" When Hedges heard Marvin had died in his sleep, he wasn't sure what to think. The timing was odd, coming on the heels of his immersion trip and the system alert....

Pierce shook his head. "His death had nothing to do with us. Poor Marv had a heart condition—a few months to live, at most. It's too bad, but now I need to be sure the system is locked down. You're sure there aren't Grid packets floatin' around out there ... just willy nilly?"

"They're all floating around out there—"

"You know what I mean ... is QUINN wallered?"

It was the same thing Hedges had wondered. Was there an issue with his network design? His code? Could there be a leak? Anything was possible. It was up to each planet to make their own interpretation of the implant and the Onculus blueprints received from the Grid. Inevitably, there would be slight variations in each system, and many opportunities for human error.

Hedges had been diligent about quantum error correction, had adjusted for noise interference, and so far, it had been effective. He had no idea why Marvin's retrieval had failed. But, he couldn't admit that to Pierce—

"Well, kid, has the system gone tits-up?"

He knew the smartest thing to do would be to stick to his story, to say the issue had been an anomaly. Just a bug. He took a deep breath and started to answer, but was saved from having to lie to Pierce, to his face this time … he was distracted by unexpected movement in one of the security feeds—the feed from the front entrance.

"I thought the orientation people were told to use the PIT entrance?"

CHAPTER 25

A nervous Oscar Rand stood outside the Pantheon building. He pulled at his shirt collar and wondered what he'd say, once inside.

All weekend, he'd been unable to stop thinking about his experiment ... and that strange file.

He'd tried many times to replicate the results, but never snagged anything more in the ion trap. Had it been a fluke? He *had* to know and—at the moment—all he had to go on were a few thumbnail images and the partial Pantheon logo.

He looked up at the brick building, at Building Q, and felt silly for being nervous; the Pantheon building was just one of many at the Ranch. One like his own.

Finally, realizing he couldn't stand there forever, Oscar went through the turnstile.

A chill swept through him as he stepped into the sleek lobby. He noticed the dark marble floor, high ceilings, a bank of elevators to the left, and a reception desk straight ahead.

The lobby was empty, cold, and quiet. A vacuum.

Odd that it would seem so deserted, Oscar thought. He glanced at the wall clock above the desk. It was nine o'clock on Monday morning and the place was as dead as the Agrippa cafeteria on gourmet food truck day.

He walked to the reception desk and stood, waiting for someone to come along. When they did, he'd ask for Marvin and—

Oscar was distracted by a photo on the desk, propped next to a phone. It was a picture of Marvin and a tall—supermodel-tall—curvaceous redhead. Obviously more than friends. Definitely not family. He picked the photo up and looked at the couple.

This creature and DeVito from the parking lot?! Seriously?

The sight of the unlikely pair made him think of Teddy. Maybe she *wasn't* out of his league....

Dream on, lover boy. You're way too deep in the Friend Zone to get out now ... you're mayor of the Zone.

He sighed and set the photo back on the desk and wondered again where everyone was. Maybe there was a different reception area, on another level ... one with actual people.

He walked to the elevators and searched for a call button. No button. He looked around for sensors, waved his arms and paced back and forth, thinking it was motion or pressure sensitive. He looked for card readers or some other form of access control, but saw nothing.

Just when he was about to give up, about to go back to his lab, one of the elevator doors slid open.

CHAPTER 26

The sudden movement in the previously dead air startled Oscar and set his nerves to jangling.

A man, dressed in black, his pants tucked into his boots, marched off the elevator and stopped in front of Oscar. He was a solid man, tall, with a military haircut. The patch on the right shoulder of his uniform was emblazoned with the Pantheon logo. SECURITY was stitched across the middle.

There was a clear, spiral wire visible behind the man's left ear.

"Can I help you?" The guard asked with a crisp, no-nonsense tone.

Oscar cleared his throat. "I'm looking for Marvin ... something."

"Marvin *something*?"

It had been a while since Oscar's interview with the human resources director and he couldn't remember the guy's last name. It was then he realized how ill-prepared he was....

"Sorry, I don't know the rest. He's in HR? I was hoping to talk with him for a minute ... gotta quick question—"

"Name?"

"Marv—", Oscar started to reply, then realized what the guard meant. "I'm Oscar Rand ... from next door." He pumped his thumb *back thataway* feeling foolish. Maybe if he turned and sprinted back to his lab, the guy'd forget the whole thing....

"What's your question?"

Oscar glanced around, grasping for something. Anything. "Well, it's kinda hard to explain—"

"Son, what is the nature of your question?"

Oscar wouldn't normally have said anything, not to a security guard, who probably didn't need a rundown of the particulars of his quantum entanglement experiment, but this wasn't a normal situation, and the guy made him want to spill his guts all over the marble floor.

"Saturday, I had this idea to be the fisherman and search for anomalous q-states, to search for quanta tagged with cryptographic signatures, and to my surprise, my ion trap seems to have caught something that had the Pantheon logo attached."

It came out in a rush and when Oscar saw the blank look on the guard's face, he felt even more ridiculous.

CHAPTER 27

"What's that kid babbling about and why the hell was the lobby unmanned?! Where's the redhead?" Pierce's boots clomped around the Ops Center, behind Hedges, all the while, he puffed on his cigar.

And, at that moment, Hedges thought the nickname Crazy Cowboy was fitting....

"She's probably in no mood to work today. Her fiancé just died, remember?" Hedges responded to his boss's rantings, but was distracted by the sight of Oscar Rand—in the Pantheon lobby, of all places.

Before Oscar told Reggie his name, Hedges knew exactly who he was. He was a legend in quantum informatics and—although Oscar couldn't possibly know it—his MIT thesis on anomalous q-state detection systems had been the inspiration for the majority of QUINN's design.

"Unbelievable," Hedges muttered and switched to the feed with the best view.

Oscar had mentioned something about snagging particles using state detection and crypto signatures. *Very interesting.*

And, apparently, it had happened on Saturday. He flashed back to the system alert, the one triggered by Marvin Trimble's retrieval failure, and wondered—

"Whatever; there still shoulda been security on the fuckin' desk." Pierce clomped and puffed.

Hedges tried to tune out the Director's ravings. He could barely hear what the two in the lobby were saying, and Pierce's bitching didn't help.

CHAPTER 28

Pierce reached over and tapped on the COMM panel, pressed SECURITY, and said, "Speak up and move closer to the kid. And, for the love of God, don't let him leave!" He sat back, eyes narrowed.

Not feeling fine.

"Move over," he said and grabbed the tablet.

He entered his username. The cursor blinked in the password field. "Shit! What's my password?"

The kid, still gawking at the lobby feed, mumbled the long string of letters and characters and, soon, Pierce was looking at his network directory, highlighted on the center screen.

He tapped on his INSURANCE folder to reveal two subfolders.

- USERS
- BLDGS

He opened the BLDGS folder and found the one for Building P.

"What'd the kid say his name was?"

"Oscar Rand."

Pierce located the folder—O. Rand, Ph.D., Physics Lab P137—and tapped on Saturday's footage.

Once the video was on-screen, he fast-forwarded until he found the section where the poofy-haired kid was talking to some girl. The two nerdlets were staring at something on an ancient laptop.

"Must be what he was talkin' about. What's that look like to you?" Pierce asked, zooming in to get a better look at the contents of the laptop's screen.

Hedges and Pierce recognized the thumbnail images at the same time.

"Cerulean!" they said and turned back to the lobby feed, their attention fully captured.

CHAPTER 29

The security guard moved closer to Oscar and raised his voice. "How did you get Pantheon property? If you have something belonging to Mr. Pierce, you should hand it over."

Again, Oscar realized how unprepared he was. He thought of the output file, back in his lab, back on his laptop's hard drive.

"Well, actually, I don't have it with me."

"Say again?"

Feeling more and more anxious, Oscar chewed on his lower lip, then, he remembered that, when Teddy had run her analysis of the data, she'd uploaded the content—the thumbnail images and the program code—to her cloud storage.

"We saved it in a cloud file."

"We?"

"Well, my friend Teddy helped me decode some of the video game walkthrough and then we noticed what looked like your logo. So, anyway, I was just dropping by today to see if I could find out where the file came from. It might help me with my experiment to pinpoint the location of the original file … I don't know…."

Oscar was aware he was rambling—a visceral reaction to discomfort, confusion, and the overwhelming desire to turn and run. To run far away from Pantheon.

They stood silently for what seemed like an eternity. The unnatural quiet of the lobby was unsettling, as was the guard's thousand-yard stare.

Oscar opened his mouth to say something—anything to fill the void—but the guard held up his hand.

Silence, soldier!

The guard said, "Yes, sir," but to whom, Oscar didn't know; the guy hadn't called *him* 'Sir', that much he knew....

The guard turned on his heel

(Tennn-hut!)

and said, "Follow me." Then, he marched toward the elevator.

CHAPTER 30

Down in the Ops Center, Hedges's mind raced. Oscar had part of the Cerulean file?! How?

He was peripherally aware of some of what Oscar was working on; the Ranch was a small world. Even though there were hundreds of labs and thousands of scientists working on different projects throughout the complex, it was a small community and there were few secrets—with one obvious exception.

How much of the Cerulean file had Oscar seen? Did he know about the Grid? Was he close to making the discovery Pantheon had made so many months ago? Anything was possible—

Pierce seemed to be thinking along the same lines.

"How the *hell* did the kid get a PIT file? Did he pluck it out of thin air? I thought QUINN was hidden—stealth mode or some shit."

"It *is* hidden. Completely. It would be impossible for anyone on the outside to access QUINN or its files," Hedges said, but in truth, he wasn't so sure. *Was* it completely hidden? With people like Oscar around, maybe not....

Hedges wondered about QUINN's integrity. Was it possible their quantum network had a leak?

Pierce again echoed his thoughts. "Well, kid, can QUINN be hacked?"

"I don't think so," Hedges said—because he still had cotton-brain and Oscar's arrival had him even more befuddled—and he regretted his choice of phrasing the moment the words left his mouth; Pierce was rigidly intolerant of uncertainty, and woe is he who appears wishy-washy....

"You don't *think* so?! You said the system issues were because of a bug. That QUINN was a hundred percent secure, and now you're sayin' it might be wallered—that with the right equipment, any knucklehead can hack it?"

"It *is* secure, when you consider the average hacker or tactical intelligence professional, but I never thought of someone like Oscar Rand ... he's not exactly a knucklehead."

"We need to see what he's got."

"He mentioned it was saved in a cloud file—"

"What're you sayin' ... it's just out there—on the *internet?!*" The last was said with the distaste of someone who'd said 'dog shit'. "Just mixed in with the public stuff? This is a nightmare," Pierce resumed his pacing: *clomp, clomp, clomp.*

"I'm sure the cloud is locked behind a password," Hedges said, and before Pierce could launch into a diatribe about passwords, he continued.

"This is good news. Look, here's Oscar, just walking through the front door, with—it seems—at least part of the Cerulean packet. I have no idea how he got it, but if we want to be sure QUINN is stable,

(and if you really want your tech library)

then who better to help us than the guy who came up with the basis for QUINN in the first place?"

That seemed to calm Pierce down and he stopped pacing.

"Fine, let's find out what the kid has." Pierce looked at his watch. "I can't have this delay. You still need to do orientation, finish up packet, and get me my tech library."

Pierce glared at Hedges then glanced up at one of the displays, the one showing the feed from the auditorium. "Isn't orientation scheduled to start?"

Hedges had forgotten all about the room full of VIPs down the hall. "I can start the introduction video; that'll keep 'em occupied ... it's usually all I do for the first hour anyway."

Pierce nodded. "Get it ready to go; I'll tell 'em you'll be in later, to answer questions." He started to leave, then turned back and glared at Hedges. "And don't talk to that kid about anything more than the weather until I get back."

Hedges queued up the orientation video and made sure it was ready for Pierce to press PLAY; soon, the VIPs would learn all about the Grid and about planet immersion travel.

Once the video was queued, he glanced around the room. There'd be hell to pay if he left anything classified out in the open.

He saw that the room was clean, except for one thing.

He swiped on his tablet and tapped at the global standby icon. Instead of showing the interior of the auditorium and the PIT rooms, the curved wall of the Ops Center was now a patchwork of displays showing the same image.

Confident the room was scrubbed, his thoughts turned to Pantheon's unexpected visitor; he had mixed feelings about Oscar being brought down to the PIT—down to *Derrick Pierce's Wacky Wondorium....*

On the one hand, he was thrilled a like mind would be joining him; if anyone had the brains to help him with a plan to stop Pierce's insane scheme, it would be Oscar Rand. On the other hand, Pierce's behavior had become more unpredictable as they neared the immersion packet deadline.

Now, with so much at stake—so much to accomplish before day's end—introducing an unknown entity into the equation was risky.

CHAPTER 31

Oscar followed the guard to the elevator. Under normal circumstances, he'd think twice about blindly obeying some random guy with no clue as to where they were headed.

But, somehow, he felt compelled to follow.

Maybe if the guard looked more like a mall cop than a guy from SEAL Team Six, maybe then he wouldn't have been so compliant. But the guy *was* intimidating and besides, Oscar had always wanted to see inside Pantheon. And, it looked as though he'd get his chance.

As to where they were going, it was a mystery—Marvin's office? Or maybe to see whoever was on the other end of that earpiece?

The elevator doors automatically slid open when they were several feet away.

"Sure, for *you*...." Oscar muttered. He stepped inside and glanced around, still unable to determine what triggered the elevator door.

The guard said, "Level Q", and the elevator zoomed down—so fast that Oscar's stomach plummeted right along with it. Then, without warning, the car stopped and shifted trajectory.

The abrupt change in direction threw him toward the side wall and he flailed around for a handrail.

The guard didn't budge. His shiny black boots remained fixed to the floor like magnets to metal.

"The elevators in *my* building sure don't have this setting," Oscar mumbled, wondering what else was different in Building Q.

Soon, the elevator came to a smooth stop and a large 'Q' glowed on the display.

Ding!

The doors slid open and the guard stood to the side.

Oscar stepped off the elevator into a brightly lit, wide hallway. It had white tile floors and—all along the corridor—there were doors, and centered over each door frame, was a red light.

Their footsteps echoed in the hall, and, as they walked, Oscar saw that some of the red lights were lit, as if there were deejays inside, or someone recording.

Where are we going? What are those rooms for? And does anyone even work aboveground at Pantheon?

There were many questions, and they were piling up, but no answers.

Oscar wondered then what Teddy was doing. She was probably in her lab—over at Neuropath. She'd get a kick out of this, he thought. She loved a good mystery. Maybe, later, he'd go over and be the one to drag *her* to lunch for a change.

He smiled and was so lost in thought— thoughts of Teddy—that he didn't realize the guard had stopped. He'd stopped so suddenly Oscar nearly plowed into the guy.

They were standing in front of a set of sliding glass doors, to the right of which was a silver plaque that read "OPS CENTER."

He looked in and saw what looked to be a command center. It was a large, oval-shaped room, sparsely furnished with a plain desk in the middle and several chairs. But what caught his attention most were the paper-thin displays plastered on the curved walls.

Experiencing a twinge of tech envy, Oscar moved closer to the wall to examine the screens. So thin were the displays, they looked like wallpaper.

He'd seen similar technology once before—at the Consumer Electronics Show in Las Vegas. What he'd seen had only been a prototype, a glimpse of what might be coming in the future. But this was the first time Oscar had seen it used in a real-world application.

The familiar Pantheon badge logo rotated on each display, and—

"Hi!"

Oscar jumped, startled by the sound of a voice coming from behind.

He turned and saw an athletic-looking guy— tall, clean-cut, around his age—and he knew who he was.

Trey Hedges.

Their research interests were so similar, that— even though they'd attended different schools and had never worked together—people were often mistaking one for the other. It had always seemed silly to Oscar; they looked nothing alike.

Whereas Oscar was short and wiry, Trey Hedges was tall and athletic. The quintessential captain-of-the-football-team kinda guy.

Through the Ranch grapevine, he'd heard that Hedges had taken the job Oscar had turned down, and, if he was there at Pantheon, they had to be working on some pretty radical stuff....

The physicist was grinning from ear to ear. He stepped forward and shook Oscar's hand. "Wow, Oscar Rand, it's so great to finally meet the legend. We were going for our doctorates at the same time and, man ... you were the talk of CalTech. I'm Trey Hedges, but everyone just calls me 'Hedges'."

Oscar grinned. The guy's enthusiasm was infectious, no doubt, but he was surprised by how excited Hedges was to see him.

"Sure, I know who you are ... *you* were the talk of MIT. I loved your paper on single-photon transmission."

"Really? Thanks! I've practically memorized your thesis on q-state detection. What have you been up to? What are you working on?" Hedges asked. "Sorry if I seem a little hyper. It's just ... we don't usually get visitors like you down here."

"Not at all. It's great to see you too. I'm dying to see what you're working on." Oscar noticed that—although the guy seemed happy—there was also a nervous energy; he seemed jumpy,

(Mr. Biggle)

and kept glancing out of the room. Kept glancing down the hall.

CHAPTER 32

Pierce looked out at all the raised hands and regretted going into the auditorium.

I'm not your orientation boy, for Chrissakes.

He'd only meant to pop in and start the video, then get back to the kids. Instead, he'd made the mistake of answering a question. One question turned into two, and now he was stuck. But, he didn't want to piss these people off, not when he was so close to his goal.

Later, he wouldn't give two shits what they thought, but for the moment, he needed to keep them happy.

He tugged at his shirt cuffs and pointed to British Prime Minister Gordon Landham.

"Why can't we do a trip from anywhere? Why do we have to come to the PIT rooms? Isn't the technology portable? It's just an implant and a simple program ... I mean, we could do it from home, right?"

Like I'd trust you out there with my tech?

"Sure, Gordy, in-home immersions will be coming soon, after global rollout. But, for now, while we're in beta test, we need to keep it here at Pantheon, in the PITs."

Having reached his limit for stupid questions, Pierce ignored the rest of the raised hands.

"Look, guys, I'm just the money man—just a traveler like you. *You* know how it is. Hedges will be in later to tell you more; he's the brains of the operation. So, sit back, watch the intro, and all will become clear. All right?"

He walked to the control panel, swiped at the screen, and the PIT introduction video began. That'll shut 'em up ... at least for an hour or so.

On the way back to the Ops Center, Pierce commed Security.

"Reggie, I need everything you can find on Oscar Rand."

He hoped leaving the kids alone hadn't been a mistake. Back when they'd watched the lobby feed of the poofy-haired kid, he noticed a look on Hedges's face, the same look he got when he was calculating something.

Usually, it was formulas for quantum hoohah, but what would the kid need to calculate while watching some random, Agrippa nerdlet?

Unless ... the drop-in *wasn't* random....

Was the surprise visit some sort of plan between the kids? Oscar had gotten hold of Pantheon data somehow. Were they up to something? Did they know each other from the outside?

Probably, he thought. Agrippa was an incestuous swarm of nerdlets and if he didn't keep a close eye on 'em, no telling what crazy schemes they'd hatch.

But, no, on second thought, he didn't think Hedges would go off the reservation. The kid knew better.

Pierce tugged at his shirt cuffs, ready to get on with it. He put on his best, Sunday-go-meetin' smile and walked into the Ops Center. "Is this our surprise guest?"

CHAPTER 33

The first thing Oscar noticed at the sound of the greeting was Hedges's immediate change in demeanor. The guy flinched and his back stiffened.

That's it! Hedges's behavior reminded him of Mr. Biggle, Oscar's boyhood cat.

Mr. Biggle would be fine and dandy—purring contentedly, licking its paws—but if Oscar's stepfather came anywhere near the cat, it would arch its back, its fur would bristle, and it would start to hiss; it was Mr. Biggle's high-alert look. And that's what Hedges looked like, standing there in the Ops Center. On high-alert.

Oscar turned to see what had raised the guy's hackles and was stunned to see Derrick Pierce, standing in the doorway.

The Pantheon Director, oddly enough, was the last person Oscar expected to see at Pantheon headquarters. Sure, the guy owned the building— pretty much owned the world—but even so, Oscar was surprised to see him.

Pierce was such a recluse, nobody ever saw him entering, or leaving, Building Q. Most people thought he never set foot on the Ranch, others thought he used a private entrance—one that circumvented the security gate and parking structure.

But there he was, standing and grinning, looking like he did in all the Pantheon press photos.

He was tall—not quite as tall as Hedges—but taller than Oscar. He wore a tailored suit and cowboy boots; he looked like a well-dressed Marlboro Man.

Oscar realized he was gawking and tried to regain a modicum of composure. He reached out and shook Pierce's hand. "Oscar Rand, sir; it's an honor to meet you."

"Honor's mine; I think you turned us down for a job here, a while back. I seem to recall HR said you were bent on joining the public sector."

Pierce stood and looked at Oscar, his expression inscrutable.

Oscar shifted uncomfortably under the Pantheon Director's gaze and wondered why such a busy man was wasting time on him. In his limited experience in the corporate world, most executives at Derrick Pierce's level avoided the minions.

Pierce took out a cigar, lit it, and casually asked, "So, what did you and Marvin talk about?"

"How did you—?" Oscar glanced at Hedges, who'd been standing back in silence, then he looked back at Pierce.

Pierce raised an eyebrow. "Our man Reggie said you wanted to see Marvin. Wanted to ask him a question."

Oscar shook his head and tried to explain. "I saw him this weekend, but we didn't speak."

"No?"

"No, we only passed each other in the parking garage. He was leaving and I was heading in. Is he around?"

"Not today, but maybe Hedges and I can help?" Pierce smiled and squinted at Oscar through the smoke haze. "What's your question?"

Oscar shifted his feet and tugged at his collar, again regretting his decision to wear the button-down shirt. What the heck had he been thinking, that morning, when he'd pulled the shirt from the dark recesses of his closet?

"Well, on Saturday, I came across something that had your logo on it. Finding out exactly where the data was from might help me determine what my experiment was doing. Maybe—"

Pierce interjected, "Can I see it?"

Oscar thought again of the file sitting on his hard drive. He supposed he could run back to Building P and get it, although, it seemed a huge waste of Derrick Pierce's time.

"It's on my computer. Should I run back to my lab and get it?"

Pierce shook his head and snapped, "No! You can't leave."

Oscar was surprised by the comment and Pierce's sudden mood shift. *Can't leave?* What the heck did *that* mean?

Pierce stepped forward and his face darkened, at the same time, Hedges retreated farther back against one of the curved walls.

The Director must have seen the look of alarm on Oscar's face, because his expression smoothed and he smiled, looking as charming as before. "I mean ... we can just grab the file from here, right?" He glanced over at Hedges, who shrugged. Then he looked back at Oscar, "You're on the Agrippa cloud?"

"No, I use my own storage."

Pierce's smile slipped again, ever so slightly, and he glanced at his watch.

Oscar couldn't figure out why Pierce was so agitated. Maybe, without knowing what data Oscar had, Pierce was angry he had anything at all. Intelligence and security *was*—after all— Pantheon's bread and butter....

Then, Oscar thought of what Pierce said about the cloud and he remembered Teddy's copy; it wasn't on *Agrippa's* cloud, but he might be able to call her and get access.

Wanting to be helpful, he blurted, "I can call a friend of mine over at Building T. She has a copy."

"Someone *else* has the file?" Pierce's eyes narrowed.

Oscar stepped back, looked up at Pierce, and mumbled, "Well, she wouldn't show it to anyone—"

When he stepped back, he was able to see more of the hallway, and he saw Branson Ross walk through a set of double doors at the end of the hallway.

What was he *doing there?*

Oscar liked Branson. Truth be told, if he ever *did* go to the dark side and join the corporate overlords, he'd have chosen Mr. Ross over Pierce. He respected what Branson did with his wealth and power, was impressed by the man's vision and philanthropic activity in the most impoverished areas of the world.

"Is that *Branson Ross?*" he asked, and glanced over at Hedges.

Hedges raised an eyebrow and shrugged, as if to say: "I know; can you believe it?"

Pierce flinched, this time his irritation was unmistakable. He looked out to see what Oscar was talking about, and quickly moved over to block the view.

"I can't discuss that," Pierce said and turned to Hedges.

"Work with our friend here ... get that file."

"Yes, sir."

Pierce turned to Oscar and, again, studied him. Finally he said, "Good, it's settled."

And, with a flash of another billion-dollar smile, he was gone.

CHAPTER 34

Now that Pierce was gone, it was just he and Hedges sitting in the Ops Center. Oscar wasn't sure what was expected of him.

"So, should I call my friend—Teddy....?"

"Teddy Lawson?" Hedges asked.

"Yeah, you know her?"

"I know *of* her; most people do, right?"

It was true, Oscar knew—that small-world effect of the Ranch.

Hedges, who had relaxed the moment Pierce left, smiled and raised an eyebrow. He nudged Oscar. "So, what's the story with you two?"

"Wha—nothing ... we're just friends—"

Thankfully, he was saved from saying more on the subject when they heard a clicking sound.

Hedges's back stiffened, again reminding Oscar of Mr. Biggle.

Oscar glanced up and noticed that a display off to the side, one slightly apart from the others, showed the words COMM: EB-II across the center of the screen.

A voice came from no particular direction. "What's my password?"

Derrick Pierce.

Hedges rolled his eyes, then glanced around the room, looking like a kid who'd just been caught sticking his tongue out at the teacher's back.

"Yeah, I saw that. Not my fault you geniuses make these passwords impossible to remember."

Hedges, through clenched teeth, recited a string of numbers and symbols.

"Thanks, kid. As you were."

There was another clicking sound and the screen went blank.

Obviously, Oscar thought, he and Hedges weren't alone in the room....

But, Hedges moved on without missing a beat, leading Oscar to believe interruptions like that were normal down there.

"Ya think Teddy's at her office?" Hedges asked.

"Probably, should we ask her to come over?" Oscar sat up, unable to keep the hopeful tone from his voice. "She'd love to see this place...."

(And you'd love to see her.)

Hedges shook his head. "No, if she stored it on Neuropath's cloud, we can get the file without disturbing her. We do a lot of work with them and can access their servers from here."

"She doesn't use Neuropath's cloud," Oscar replied, knowing that most people at the Ranch eschewed the Agrippa-hosted cloud storage in favor of their own secure servers. It was frowned upon, but they were a paranoid bunch, and now—he could see—rightfully so.

Hedges nodded, seeming to know the same.

There was another click and again, COMM: EB-II appeared onscreen.

"We need that file; COMM her office, but remember her clearance level."

It took a moment for Pierce's comment to register in Oscar's brain.

COMM her office?! Pierce had the whole complex wired—or just the Neuropath building?

Oscar knew that Teddy suspected some of her consulting gigs were for Pantheon, but just how entangled was Neuropath with the conglomerate? And why would they have Teddy's office wired?

"Yes, sir," Hedges said. He shot a rueful look at Oscar, then tapped on a file labeled BUILDING R.

He typed TEDDY LAWSON into a search field and opened the single result. Then, a dialog box appeared with the options COMM, VIDEO, MUTE, UNMUTE, CLIENT, and MONITOR. Another set of options appeared below the main icons: 2-way and 1-way.

Hedges chose the option for COMM 2-way and VIDEO 1-way and the center display showed the familiar interior of Teddy's office.

It was empty.

Then, Oscar saw Teddy's profile in the background, through the window between her office and lab.

Strains of Bob Marley's "No Woman, No Cry" filtered through the COMM speakers, and they could see Teddy swaying in time to the music.

To get a better angle, Hedges clicked on another feed: T. LAWSON, NEUROPATH LAB T169.

Their field of view changed and now they could clearly see Teddy; the video was crisp and clear, it was as if they were watching her through a window.

Teddy danced over to the wall to her right and flipped on a light switch. The wall lit up to reveal several dozen brain scans.

The scans were mainly blue, with areas of each brain lit up in splotches of red, green, or yellow. She studied the scans, all the while, her hips swayed.

Although Oscar couldn't complain about the view, what he was witnessing was disturbing, to say the least. Stalkery. And, he couldn't help but wonder if *his* lab was wired....

"Teddy Lawson," Hedges said, but not loudly enough to be heard over the music.

He said her name again, louder this time.

CHAPTER 35

Oscar saw Teddy jump at the sound of her name and they heard her yell, "Holy shit, Batman!"

She whipped around and scrambled to turn the music off. Her surprise turned to confusion when she didn't see anyone in the lab.

"Is someone there?" She called and walked toward her office, past the wall of brain scans. As she walked, she pulled her long hair up and into a ponytail.

"Helloooooo?"

"Jerkytits," Oscar said, hoping a friendly voice would put a buffer on what he was sure would be the creepy realization she was being watched. "I'm over at Pantheon. They've got a COMM system and—" He stopped when Hedges nudged him, hard, in the ribs.

Then, they heard a *click*, and Hedges tensed up, going into Mr. Biggle-mode.

The side display flickered briefly and COMM: EB-II appeared. Then, there was another click and the screen went blank. Hedges relaxed, but remained alert.

"Numbnuts?" Teddy said and stopped short, with one foot in her lab and one in her office.

She looked around at the ceiling, at the walls, and out the window. "I didn't realize this building had an intercom? You're at Pantheon? Did you find out about that video game file? What the f—"

"Teddy, I know this is weird, but just listen for a second. I can't go into detail, but what I need for you to do is get the file we worked on this weekend. Remember? It's still on your cloud, right?"

She nodded. "Sure. So it *was* Pantheon's, eh? Was it a video game or what?"

"I really wish I could say," *and even if I could, I know about as much as you,* "but, I can't."

She was silent for a moment, then said, "Whatever you need. So, should I bring it over?"

Hedges shook his head at Oscar, and reached over and pressed MUTE. He glanced at the blank display, the one to the left, seemed about to say something, thought for a minute, then reached forward and tapped UNMUTE.

"Teddy, it's Trey Hedges here. Can you just get the file from your personal server ... then be sure you scrub any trace of it?"

They saw her glance at her office, at her desk, at her tablet. "My server? Oscar, you *told* them about that?" Her eyes narrowed.

Oscar knew that look. *Shit.*

"Teddy, trust me on this...."

She didn't move and Oscar could tell she was irritated. He didn't blame her.

Finally she said, "All right, but you owe me...."

She went into her office and Hedges switched the feed. Now, they could see her at her desk. She tapped at her tablet for a moment, then sat back and said, "Now what?"

Hedges, who'd been typing at the same time, looked up and replied, "OK, you should see a new folder in your Neuropath directory."

She shook her head, her mouth fixed in a straight line, and Oscar knew she was seething.

"So, does everyone over there know what color panties I'm wearing?" She jabbed at her tablet, then said, "Okay, I see it—a file called PANTHEON?"

Oscar had to admire her restraint. If it had been anyone else asking her to do this, anyone other than Oscar, she'd have shut it down in a heartbeat.

"Okay … it's done." She sat back and crossed her arms. "Now what?"

"Thank you, Teddy," Oscar said, wishing he could say more.

"That's *it*? That's all I get?"

"Teddy, I'll see you later, okay?" Oscar felt lame; it *was* lame.

"Fine, but, yeah; you owe me a *huge* explanation for this."

Oscar hoped he could explain. Later.

But his sense of unease was growing with every moment he remained at Pantheon—with every moment he spent in the bizarre underground with the tense fraidy-cat and the intense Crazy Cowboy.

Now that the Teddy Cam was off, the displays returned to the Pantheon logo. Then, the COMM display flickered on.

"Well?" Pierce asked.

"We got it; I'm just checking to see if it's the Cer—" Hedges cut himself short, then looked at Oscar. "I'll see if it's the file."

"I'll be right there.

CHAPTER 36

Pierce ducked out of Edit Bay-II. What he'd witnessed between nerd and nerdletta had given him an idea. The poofy-haired kid obviously had a thing for the girl, and that knowledge might come in handy.

A quick background check on Teddy Lawson told him she was some sort of neuro genius and her employer had done work on the PIT software: she'd been one of the key consultants on some of the Onculus code.

He made a quick call to the security office, then headed back to the Ops Center.

If the file the kid had found turned out to be the Cerulean packet, they might find out why Trimble's trip had gone tits-up on Saturday. And Pierce wondered if the kid had lied to him, when he'd said the system alert was just a bug....

Pierce had already spent too much time on the issue and he was ready to get on with the more important business of the day—his tech day.

He walked into the Ops Center. "Well?"

Hedges nodded. "It's the file."

Pierce turned to Oscar. No more fuckin' around; it was time to get serious with the kid.

"How did you get my file? Is this something you do a lot ... hack other people's systems?"

CHAPTER 37

Oscar stumbled backward, surprised by Pierce's malevolent look.

"I—what? No! No, sir. This is the first time my experiment worked ... I don't know how it happened. That's why I'm here. I tried to replicate my results, but got nowhere ... believe me; I had no intention of hacking Pantheon—"

"But, you must have some idea how you got our file...."

Given the sudden shift in Pierce's mood, the urgency to get the file fast, and given that he wouldn't let Oscar leave Pantheon to go to his lab, it was becoming clear that the file was not just some video game walkthrough.

What had Pierce said—that Hedges should remember Teddy's clearance level? Maybe it was black-ops, high-octane, military intelligence, the file fragments he'd found.

"I got it when I ran an anomalous quantum-state search."

Oscar was relieved when Hedges nodded, as if the explanation made perfect sense.

Pierce, however, scrunched his face up and looked even more annoyed.

CHAPTER 38

"In English, for chrissake," Pierce said, then saw the look on the kid's face. He always forgot how sensitive nerdlets could be.

He just wanted to know how the kid ended up with his file, that's all: he didn't need a physics lesson. He got plenty of that twaddle from Hedges.

Somehow, he managed to plaster on a smile. "I'm sure you didn't *intentionally* try to hack us, but it's important I know exactly how you got it. As I'm sure you can appreciate, we're dealing with issues of national security."

Hedges stepped forward. "Maybe Oscar can help me troubleshoot the leak? If we tell him," Hedges glanced at Oscar, "he might be able to help. I mean, he found *this*, after all."

Pierce looked from one kid to the other and wondered again if this was all part of a plan the two of them had hatched—some scheme to stop him from getting his tech library. If so, he couldn't see what it might be....

Maybe the kid had a point. If Oscar had managed to pick up one of their files, using some sort of quantum hoohah, then it might be smart to have him stick around a while.

Pierce looked down the hall toward the auditorium.

Orientation was underway and soon, the natives would get restless. Besides, the kid thought it was a video game or whatnot; so maybe, it wouldn't hurt to keep him around a while longer. At least, long enough to be sure things were under control.

Still, he hated having outsiders this close to QUINN. He didn't even like to share it with the users who'd been invited. The ones who paid for the privilege.

CHAPTER 39

Hedges watched Pierce and could see the Director was deciding whether to cut Oscar loose or to keep him around.

He *had* to let Oscar stay; Hedges needed an ally, now more than ever. Somehow, he needed to show Oscar what was at stake.

Given one or two hints, it probably wouldn't be too difficult to get him to connect the dots. QUINN *was*, after all, Oscar's concept; his doctoral thesis had served as the blueprint for its framework.

No matter how much he wanted to, Hedges couldn't just blurt out: *"We found an intergalactic network with a library of inventions and now Pierce wants to keep the billions of years of technology to himself!"*

But, there had to be something else he could do—something subtle. Then, he got an idea.

It'd be risky, but he decided to go for it; he was tired of sitting around doing nothing. He didn't know when he'd get another opportunity like the one that had fallen in his lap when Oscar Rand turned up on their doorstep.

CHAPTER 40

With interest, Oscar watched the exchange between Hedges and Pierce.

Pierce was pacing and seemed to be mulling something over. Every so often, he'd stop and glance between Oscar and Hedges, then he'd resume pacing.

Hedges was looking down at something in his lap, something partly hidden under the desk. He looked like a student texting in the back row of a classroom, one on alert to when the teacher was about to turn around.

At that moment, Hedges looked up and caught Oscar's eye. He glanced at Pierce, whose back was turned, then tilted his head at the wall of displays.

Oscar followed his gaze. The screen closest to him flickered on and an image appeared. An image he instantly recognized.

It was so unexpected—seemed so out of place outside his lab, outside his imagination—that all he could do was stare and move closer to the display, to try to get a better look.

It couldn't be what he thought it was. Could it? The q-state detection schematic from his thesis?

He studied the figure and saw the familiar layout of the ion trap. Unlike Q-bert's single-zone ion trap, this one was separated into four storage regions. But—by far the most interesting section of the schematic—was the ionospheric collector array.

Oscar's had also included an array, but his had been modest in comparison to the one onscreen.

He noted, with more than a little envy, that *this* array was a constellation of collectors, apparently attached to satellites in high-Earth orbit. The things he could do with that equipment....

The collection capacity of such a large array would function as a massive, cosmic dust collector, scooping and filtering particles. Then, the particles could be analyzed and filtered for, Oscar assumed, unnatural q-states.

He didn't see any notations on the schematic for ground-based receivers. Could they be using entanglement to transfer data trapped by the collectors?

Seeing the schematic gave Oscar a taste of something he'd wondered about since turning down the Pantheon job: exactly what kind of equipment he'd have access to.

Now he knew. Trey Hedges was one lucky son of a bitch—a jumpy and nervous cat, maybe—but lucky, nonetheless.

Oscar was happy he'd decided to go to Building Q. Seeing the schematic went a long way to explaining how he'd plucked the data out of the air; it looked like he and Pantheon were using the same principles of q-state detection, trapping, and cryptography—

Just then, Pierce—who'd been pacing and chomping on his cigar—turned and finally noticed Oscar's distraction. Noticed that he was staring at one of the displays.

Pierce followed his gaze and saw the schematic.

"Idiot!" He yelled and lunged at Hedges. He reached under the desk and wrenched the tablet from the startled physicist's grasp. Pierce swiped and jabbed at icons until, finally, the schematic disappeared.

"Was that ... a q-state detection schematic?" Oscar asked, his mind racing, scrambling to fit the pieces together.

Pierce glared at Hedges, who flinched back in his chair.

"Sorry, sir, I don't know how that happened."

"That was eyes-only," Pierce said, this time, directing his ire toward Oscar, as if it was *his* fault the image had appeared.

"Sorry," Oscar said, and backed away. The look on the Director's face was chilling. The last time he'd seen a look like that was at the zoo, when he'd gotten too close to a tiger's cage. The tiger had whipped around and stared at him, its nostrils flaring, sniffing the air, like it smelled raw meat.

"I'm just fascinated, that's all. It's almost exactly as I laid out in my thesis. There are a few modifications, but, yeah ... I mean, I guess it could work. There might be issues with noise interference or leakage...." he trailed off and backed as far away from Pierce as he could until he ran out of real estate, until his back was against the curved wall.

The file fragments with the crisp alien landscapes and partial Pantheon logo flashed through his mind.

"Leakage?" Pierce asked and stopped advancing, his angry expression turned into something else, something Oscar couldn't identify.

Then, he noticed a similar expression on Hedges's face.

What the hell's going on down here?

CHAPTER 41

Pierce's anger faded. The poofy-haired kid had seen something.

If QUINN had a leak, they needed to get it plugged. He looked at his watch. Almost ten o'clock: still early. The deadline for submission to the Grid was four o'clock, but there was no time to relax—there was still plenty to do and there wasn't a thing in the world that would keep him from his goal.

Pierce made a decision: he'd let the kid in on their little secret. Besides, he could see that the cover story of a video game file was quickly losing its shine.

Now that Oscar had spotted the schematic, he figured he may as well give up the goods. He'd deal with the new kid later, besides, if he got outta line, he had insurance.

He *always* had insurance. He tugged at his shirt cuffs and turned to Hedges. "Pull up the auditorium feed and see where they're at."

The kid stared at him, wall-eyed, looking like Pierce had asked him to pull down his pants and wave 'howdy' with his ding-a-ling.

"Really?!"

Pierce nodded, "Yup, *really*. It'll be the quickest way to get him up to speed; if he sees the whole operation, you two can put your freak brains together and get 'er fixed."

CHAPTER 42

Perfect! Hedges was thrilled he'd "accidentally" let the schematic appear. He glanced at Oscar, who—he could see—had already started down the path to figuring some of it out, but there was no way he'd guess what QUINN had found.

Before Pierce could change his mind, Hedges scrambled to pull up the orientation feed.

He set it to display on all screens and was surprised to see that the intro video had only progressed to the section covering immersion packet selection; it seemed as if they'd been in the Ops Center forever, but there was still plenty of content for Oscar to view.

They stood in front of the curved wall of displays and listened to the female narrator, who spoke over a backdrop of the Grid user interface.

Hedges, having sat through the video several times before, recognized the tutorial on browsing immersion packets and preference-matching algorithms.

"—and, in addition to filtering for planets with native sensations like echolocation and synesthesia, you'll receive packet suggestions based on your unique neuromap. The suggestion algorithms scan trillions of neuroprofiles and, when another being's profile is at least an 85% match to yours, you'll receive suggestions based on *their* favorites. Those packets will automatically appear in your suggestion queue. This matching system makes browsing the overwhelming number of immersion packets an intuitive process. The suggestion algorithms have been perfected over billions of years, and we think you'll find the offerings relevant to your individual tastes."

Pierce nodded and said, "It's getting to the good stuff. Flip off the feed and let's go; he'll get a much better view in the auditorium." With that, he left the Ops Center.

Hedges cleared the displays and turned to follow, but Oscar continued to stare at the blank screens. He didn't seem to realize that Pierce had left and that Hedges was waiting.

"I know, believe me, it's a lot to absorb, but he's right ... you'll get a much better sense of it in there."

Oscar just stared and muttered, "Sense of what, exactly? It's not a video game walkthrough ... that file I found—"

"No. It's not," Hedges smiled.

He could almost hear the wheels turning in Oscar's head and he remembered *his* first time, back when Uri had explained everything. Of course, Hedges had been primed—having found the Grid beacon—but still, he remembered what it was like.

But, the human brain is malleable. It adjusts quickly to a new status quo, and then, what was once mind-bending becomes sort of ... familiar.

Hedges glanced out and down the hall.

An impatient Derrick Pierce stood outside the auditorium door, tapping his foot and staring back toward the Ops Center.

Hedges touched Oscar's elbow. "Come on; you don't wanna miss this...."

As they walked out, he leaned over and whispered, "Besides, I need you to see everything. I need your help."

"Wha—?"

"Not now. Later."

CHAPTER 43

"About time," Pierce grumbled when they arrived at the auditorium doors. He guided them down to the front row and asked, "What were you two whispering about?"

"Noth—," Hedges started to respond, but Pierce interrupted.

"Quiet and let him watch. You're up next."

As Oscar made his way down the aisle, he saw Branson Ross, sitting in the center of the auditorium. To Branson's left sat the Sultan of Brunei, and to his right, sat Prince Henri of Luxembourg.

Oscar was only peripherally aware of how strange it was to see such a congregation of wealth and power in one room, and his mind flashed back to the empty lobby. Wouldn't there be heightened security with so many world leaders amassed in one location?

But, that mystery would have to remain unexplored. Such Earthly concerns paled in comparison to what he'd just heard and one thing kept replaying in his mind: "The suggestion algorithms have been perfected over billions of years."

Billions of years?! Perfected by whom?

Worried he was missing the answers, he took his seat in the front row—between Hedges and Pierce—and watched the rest of the video.

After the packet selection tutorial, the narrator gave a brief overview of something called an Onculus, and Oscar finally learned the purpose of the rooms with the red lights.

There was an animation showing a person in one of the rooms and Oscar watched, fascinated, as the Onculus arm descended. The narrator explained how the user's implant retrieved an immersion packet and replayed the original recording.

As he listened, he couldn't help thinking of Teddy. She often spoke of the future of bioengineering, of a brain-computer interface—an implant—but she always said such advancements were a long way off.

And yet, here he sat, listening to a description of such an interface—one implanted in the thalamus via insulin-like growth factors, able to cross the blood-brain barrier. It acted as a gateway, a toggle switch telling one being's brain to playback another's experience. To play it back like a lucid dream.

After the Onculus demonstration and packet immersion information, there was a brief mention of an intergalactic cooperative of billions of planets sharing knowledge and technology—something called "the Grid". Oscar hoped there would be more details, but too soon, the video ended; there had been no mention of how they'd discovered the supposed "intergalactic cooperative" in the first place....

Now that the presentation was over, there was a buzz of chatter throughout the auditorium, but Oscar barely noticed. He was trying hard to piece together what he'd heard.

Was he to believe that Pantheon had found an alien internet, one that enabled sentient beings to experience somatosensory stimuli and total immersion in an exoplanetary landscape? If so, he thought wryly, that would be a whole new way to look at someone's vacation video.

He considered—not for the first time since sitting down—the possibility it was all an elaborate hoax. It could be. Easily.

Oscar looked around the room at the world leaders and billionaires, at the presidents and prime ministers, and he thought they'd be plum targets for such a hoax; people who'd seen and done it all. People who needed to up the ante: needed bigger and better toys, more adrenaline, more stimulation. More intensity. For them, novel experiences would be hard to come by.

So, if Mr. Pierce was charging for the privilege of using a revolutionary, planet immersion technology, then the hoax idea was plausible— and lucrative.

But, Oscar *wanted* to believe there was an entire universe of communication and shared experiences going on. If he didn't, what the hell was he doing pinging particles all day?

He wondered how many others had sat through the same presentation; how many others had been seduced into traveling the Grid—

Oscar was pulled from his musings when he saw that Hedges had left his seat and was standing center stage.

"I'm sure you all have questions," Hedges said. He glanced down at Pierce, who tapped his watch. "We have time for just a few."

Hands shot up around the room and Hedges nodded toward the right side of the auditorium. "Yes, Mr. Shorson?"

Oscar turned to see Mr. Shorson, who was tapping at a touchpad jutting from the arm of his chair.

"Most of the immersion packets are grayed out. Why?"

Oscar glanced down at his own chair and noticed a silver button on the arm, like the RECLINE button on an airplane seat. He pressed the button.

A small monitor rose out of the arm and switched on to reveal a user interface.

He tapped on an icon labeled PIT USER MENU and a login screen appeared, prompting him for a username and password. Thwarted, Oscar sat back and listened while Hedges responded to the question.

CHAPTER 44

Hedges had conducted several orientations, and inevitably, the questions were the same. It allowed him to run on semi-autopilot; gave his mind a chance to run scenarios in the back of his mind ... about ways Oscar might be able to help—

"Not all packets are available because we're running in demo mode," he explained. "As a new Grid member, Earth is only granted access to a fraction of the planet immersion library. Once we submit our *own* immersion packet, we'll be granted full access."

Hedges looked pointedly at Pierce, then raised his voice. "As mentioned earlier, the Grid prides itself on being completely open and accessible to *all* beings throughout the Universe. Reciprocity is the cornerstone of the co-op."

His words had fallen on deaf ears. Pierce wasn't paying attention; he was looking down at his tablet.

It wouldn't have mattered, even if he'd heard. Pierce had made it clear during their recording tour that he didn't give a crap about the Grid's philosophy of sharing. He was willing to risk

Earth's access by locking everyone out of the tech library.

Hedges sighed and nodded to Gloria Turing, owner of Platinum Networks, the world's largest entertainment and communications company.

"Yes, Ms. Turing?"

"My question is about the suggestion algorithm. I see that 51 Peg Ab is in my suggestion queue and, in the Viscera menu, EUPHORIA is bold and in all caps—"

Another user interjected. "No, for that planet, the main sensation is PAIN."

Hedges nodded. "Actually, you're *both* right; two different beings, on 51 Peg Ab, recorded the same script. Each one experienced a different visceral reaction to the same stimuli. Given that, you may discover that your experience of a planet may be entirely different from that of another Grid user."

Another question, this time from the back row.

"How many versions of each planet script are there?"

"It depends on the neuro-fitness of a planet's beings. Unlike playback, recording an immersion can't be done by just any native brain. The information processing hardware—the motherboard, if you like: the synapses, neural connections, neurotransmitters—all components and connections need to be pristine to record. That's why, on some planets, there may only be one or two versions of the same script."

"So, where's Earth's packet? I don't see it in the library."

Hedges glanced at Pierce, wondering how much he could reveal about the submission deadline.

But, Pierce was still engrossed in whatever he was looking at on his tablet, so Hedges continued. "As a matter of fact, it'll be uploaded today. Once it's approved by the Gridmaster, it'll be open to the entire Grid."

"Who recorded our packet? And what was the script?"

"I was lucky enough to be Earth's first recorder. By day's end, you'll be able to review our packet and look at the sites we visited, at the viscera we included. You'll recognize all the greatest hits—Machu Picchu, the Pyramids, the Great Barrier Reef, the Grand Canyon—"

"How did you decide what to record? What to include in our Packet? How does Pantheon know it's the best representation of what Earth has to offer?"

Hedges paused, distracted by Pierce, who was twirling a finger in the air like he was winding up a miniature lasso.

Wrap it up.

"Sorry guys, that's all we have time for. For most of the frequently asked questions, you can consult the PIT User Guide, but remember," he said, raising his voice to be heard over the chatter and the rustle of belongings being gathered. "Per your NDA, you're prohibited from sharing this information with a non-user; not a hint of the Grid leaves the underground. Thanks for coming ... you're free to login to the PIT system to schedule your first immersion!"

CHAPTER 45

Hedges was glad orientation was over. As far as he was concerned, there was only one VIP in the audience.

All throughout the video and during the question and answer period, he'd wondered what was going through Oscar's mind; he'd only seen half the video, so he'd surely be left with many unanswered questions, such as, how they'd found the Grid in the first place....

Hedges walked to the edge of the stage and jumped down, landing in front of Pierce and Oscar. He overheard Pierce ask Oscar what he thought of the presentation.

Oscar was silent for a moment, seeming unsure of how to respond. Finally, he shrugged and said, "It's a lot to digest, Mr. Pierce."

Pierce looked disappointed by Oscar's less than enthusiastic response. He glanced between Hedges and Oscar, then he tugged at his shirt cuffs.

Hedges recognized the calculating gleam in the Director's eyes and he didn't like the look, not one bit.

Pierce leaned back in his chair and grinned at Oscar. "Well, I should confess that our little project—QUINN, the Grid, the immersions—is all a simulation … as I'm sure a smart guy like you has figured out. But, even if it isn't the real thing, we'd still appreciate your help with some system issues. Ya think you can do that for us?"

It took a moment for Pierce's words to register, then, cold fingers of dread squeezed Hedges's heart. Pierce was trying to pass it off as a fake! A simulation. Oscar's not going to believe that—

But Oscar laughed.

"I thought it seemed a little far-fetched." He looked at Hedges and smiled. "But, wow, wouldn't that be cool if there really *was* an alien internet out there."

But there is! Hedges wanted to scream. He didn't know what Pierce was up to. He was sure that, back in the Ops Center, Pierce had decided to tell Oscar everything. But now....

Hedges looked at Pierce, who seemed to be studying him, waiting for his reaction. The Director looked pleased, vindicated somehow. It was as if Pierce had read his mind, had realized that Hedges was working on a plan to tell Oscar about the tech library.

Now, anything Hedges told Oscar—about a conspiracy to classify portions of the Grid—would sound like the ravings of a madman.

Pierce locked eyes with Hedges, seeming to reach into his soul and feed off the hopelessness he found there. Then, he nodded and smirked.

"Go on. Get to the Grid room and get QUINN patched up; we're running out of time."

"What's the hurry?" Oscar asked. Innocent, unsuspecting.

Pierce half-smiled and said, "Some of our investors—I'm sure you noticed the VIPs here— gave us a deadline of this afternoon to be fully operational."

Oscar nodded, "I know how investors can be, believe me."

While Oscar and Pierce shared a laugh, Hedges stood, feeling miserable, his seedlings of hope dying before they'd had a chance to take root.

Now, instead of gaining a potential ally, all he'd succeeded in doing was to push an innocent bystander into the path of Pierce's crazy train.

CHAPTER 46

Pierce looked at his watch: eleven fifteen. If the kids hurried and got the system issues handled and the packet ready for his review, they'd be ahead of schedule. It couldn't have gone any better with the poofy-haired kid.

Pierce was pleased with his sudden inspiration—to say it was all a simulation. Now, he didn't have to worry so much about letting an outsider see the operation.

And, if Hedges had been getting ideas about derailing the works—about telling Oscar about the tech library—if he whined about the open sharing bullshit, he'd sound like a nattering loon, like one of those conspiracy nut jobs always spreading rumors around Agrippa.

Pierce was about to leave the auditorium when he spotted Senator Walter Higgs, seated several rows back, rubbing his forehead and tapping at a touchscreen.

He went over and sat down.

"Hey, Wally. What's the good word? Have you chosen a packet?"

Wally looked up and nodded, "I gotta admit, Derrick, you've outdone yourself."

"Glad you approve. Which one did you pick?"

"Zoller-3b."

"Good choice; they have the ability to read minds. It's somethin' else. I remember—"

"How do you know? I thought you couldn't—"

"Before!" Pierce snapped.

For fuck's sake.

Wally had only been a user for a blink of an eye, and the others had wasted no time in spilling all the gory details of Pierce's implant malfunction.

Pierce managed a tight smile. He had to be careful; he didn't want Wally to storm off in a huff, not before getting his uptight ass into an immersion room.

"By the way, how did the Geneva summit go last night? Did you Masters of the Universe patch up the world?"

Wally shrugged and glanced away, seeming to avoid eye contact. "We tried...."

Pierce stood and pulled out a fresh cigar. "Well, enjoy your trip." He turned to leave, but the Senator reached out and grabbed his arm.

"I've been getting headaches. Last night, had one so bad I almost missed an important meeting. Are you sure this thing's safe?" Wally asked, rubbing his bald head.

Pierce smiled and waved his cigar. "Absolutely. It's perfectly normal. After a while, you won't even notice."

"I hope not."

"You'll be fine; just get in there and enjoy."

Pierce left the auditorium and entered the hallway, glancing to see how many red lights were lit. He was pleased to see that most of the new users had already gone into an immersion.

Names appeared to the left of each door—next to each room number—scrolling across digital displays. Displays that looked like mini tickers from the old New York Stock Exchange.

He hoped Wally nutted up and got into a room of his own....

CHAPTER 47

Oscar was awed; he felt like he was standing in the middle of the Universe.

He and Hedges were down the hall from the auditorium, in the Grid room—a room the size of several airplane hangars.

But the only thing in the room was a hologram of a Hubble-II image of the Milky Way galaxy. Standing in the middle of the hologram was like being embraced by a hundred billion stars and planets.

Hedges held a tablet, one that showed a mini version of the hologram. He tapped an icon labeled GRID OVERLAY.

The resulting display reminded Oscar of a satellite image of a city, atop which a grid of streets and highways was overlaid.

This grid, however, was set over the familiar spiral galaxy. Some lines intersected, some were connected by brighter dots, and some lines were disconnected, linked to nothing.

Oscar noticed the brighter dots were labeled with planet names and—next to some of the names—were mini file icons.

Hedges said, "Find a planet you like and tap on its folder."

Oscar walked through the hologram. As he moved, he noticed a slight jitter. For a brief moment, a portion of the Pantheon logo could be seen through the stars and planets, then the jitter was gone, and the rift was repaired.

Hedges also noticed the disturbance and explained. "Ignore any jitters. We're still tweaking the projection system—we get a strange interference. Maybe from something above ... in Building R."

"Building R?" Oscar thought about his sideways elevator ride. "How far do the elevators go—how far away from Building Q?"

"All around the complex."

"Why?"

Hedges glanced at the far wall, at the same type of COMM screen that was in the Ops Center.

The display was silent, blank. As was Hedges.

Oscar decided the sideways elevator and an apparent underground tunnel system were the least interesting things at the moment. He turned back to the hologram and wandered through, taking his time.

He recognized several exoplanets, including HD 142b, the Upsilon Andromedae system, the 55 Cancri system, Tau Bootis b, and 51 Peg b. Finally, he spotted his favorite planet of the Milky Way—Kepler-16b—and he tapped on its folder.

Now, superimposed over the galaxy image, was the same interface he'd seen back in the Ops

Center, complete with links to reviews, user ratings, and screenshots.

"Okay. Now," Hedges said, "you can read trip reviews, view thumbnails of the natives and of the planet's landscape, view Viscera options, add the packet to your wish list, or find related immersion packets."

Oscar reached out and tapped on VISCERA. The sensation and perception options for Kepler-16b included echolocation and the ability to fly.

It was a detailed interface, he thought, but now, it was easy to see it couldn't possibly be extraterrestrial; it could only be—as Pierce had said—a simulation.

The user interface was too much like any other on Earth; it shouldn't be easy to understand. Shouldn't be easy to read the planet labels and menus.

If it truly were an intergalactic interface—one targeted toward all manner of sentient beings throughout the Universe—it wouldn't look like it had come from the mind of any UIX designer in New Delhi, Seattle, or San Jose.

Most glaringly obvious were the planet names, a nomenclature that could only be attributed to the International Astronomical Union.

Surely an alien wouldn't *also* come up with the name *Kepler-16b*—same as the IAU....

"It's detailed," Oscar admitted, "but it would be more believable if it weren't so ... Earth-centric."

CHAPTER 48

Hedges balked at the comment, but it wasn't Oscar's fault that he believed it was a simulation. If only he could be convincing enough in his explanation of why the Grid looked the way it looked—why it had an easy to understand interface—he might be able to plant a seed of doubt in Oscar's mind. One that overrode Pierce's previous claim.

And, if Pierce happened to be eavesdropping, as usual, it would just sound as if Hedges was explaining the Grid operation so that Oscar could help with troubleshooting....

"The Grid translates universal concepts into something that can be understood by all beings. Every interface on every planet will look slightly different—or *completely* different—depending on the conceptualization of its beings."

Oscar raised an eyebrow and shook his head, so Hedges offered a more concrete example.

"Take libraries, for instance. 'Library' is a concept: a structure to store and organize information. When I think of the word 'library', I get a specific image, and when you think of 'library', you also get an image, and we probably don't see the same thing, in our mind's eye. Mine may look like my hometown library; yours may look like the library at MIT. Regardless, we each understand the 'library' concept; we know what the label means and its function. The Grid takes our neuromaps and converts our concepts and constructs into visual representations; constructs which can be reinterpreted by any target being's neuromap."

Hedges paused to see if Oscar was following. Oscar nodded, so he continued.

"A core set of concepts is used to translate the entire Grid infrastructure so it can be universally understood. Over billions of years, the translations evolved to include representations of time, beginning, end, part, whole, growth, evolution, entropy, life, death, near, and far. There are many other concepts that bring intelligent life forms—no matter the origin—to a common understanding and experience. Language is another construct: one of symbols and phonemes used to communicate and share information. The translator reads all constructs on the Grid, finds the neural locus of each concept, and converts it to an easily understood visual representation, customized for each planet." Hedges turned away from the hologram. "Of course, that's a gross oversimplification, but I think you get the gist."

"Do you only have this image—only the Milky Way? I mean, is this all of the Grid?"

Instead of answering, Hedges tapped on his tablet and the hologram zoomed out.

He continued to tap until the zoom out was complete, until they could no longer make out the Milky Way; it was lost among billions of other galaxies and galaxy clusters.

To Oscar, it was like *Where's Waldo?* on an intergalactic scale.

"What you now see is only a small section—a fraction of our visible universe—this swath covers approximately two billion light years of area. You need to click on the tabs to see other sections and still, there are more tabs beyond the visible horizon. We don't know how many tabs there are—I presume it goes on forever. You'd be long dead before you've opened every one."

CHAPTER 49

Oscar looked at the tabs running across the top of the hologram and noticed the continuation arrows.

"But, *you* designed this, so of course you'd know how many tabs there are—", he mused, but then, he was distracted by an error in the holographic projection, in the area of a galaxy that should no longer be there.

He pointed to the area, at a red planet.

"This area is the site of SN-2012aw, a supernova from about three years ago. It shouldn't have a folder next to it; there wouldn't be any immersion packet creation going on there." Oscar chuckled. "In fact," he said, glancing around the hologram, "you may have many such events that should be removed from the sim...."

Hedges explained the discrepancy. "The Grid keeps an archive of all packets. You can go on an immersion even if the planet's gone. It's like the internet's *Wayback Machine*, but instead of looking at an old copy of a website, you're looking at a planet and civilization that's no more."

Oscar had to admire how faithfully the guy was sticking to the script. More than that, he was impressed by the amount of detail and thought that had gone into the sim design.

"Your designers have thought of everything."

Hedges got a look then, one that Oscar interpreted as impatience.

It *was* taking a while to explain everything, and Pierce had made it clear they were on a deadline. One imposed by investors, the VIPs from the auditorium.

Oscar was ready to move on. The hologram was cool and all, but he was more interested in their quantum detection system. He couldn't stop thinking about the collector array from the schematic. "So, what about this system issue?"

Hedges glanced at the clock on the wall, and nodded, looking grim. "Yeah, we should probably get to that. I'm hoping you'll have some ideas. Remember that schematic you saw in the Ops Center?"

Oscar thought of his own experiment—of the new tweaks he'd made on Saturday. "Sure, it reminded me of my own q-state detection design."

Hedges looked sheepish. "Yeah, it should. I hope you don't mind; I cribbed a lot of the QUINN design from your thesis."

"I thought so! When I saw that—"

"Yeah, sorry."

"Don't be! Mostly, I'm just envious of that collector array. Is that real or just drawn in for the sim?"

"It's real. An array we have up in the ionosphere, in high-Earth orbit. Pantheon was able to piggyback a collector onto every GPS satellite launched over the past several years."

"You're kidding? Have you found anything?"

Hedges glanced over at the COMM display and jutted his chin out, looking defiant. For a moment, the fraidy-cat was gone. "Yeah. I found the Grid beacon."

Oscar smiled. "Oh right ... the Grid beacon."

"Yes, the *Grid beacon*. Almost immediately after the array was complete, after the last satellite settled into its orbit, we captured an encoded crystal."

"And what did this beacon say?"

"It was tagged with a cryptographic key and cosmic coordinates. Turns out, there's a whole mess of beacon particles out there, just waiting for intelligent civilizations to reach the point at which they can detect such particles."

Oscar thought of the Drake equation. What Hedges was describing—the beacons, quanta encoded with signatures—sounded so much like his own hypotheses....

Maybe it *was* real. Maybe Pantheon *had* found a beacon.

Hedges seemed to believe what he was saying—didn't sound like he was talking about a sim. The guy was too earnest and didn't strike Oscar as that good a liar.

Either way, Oscar couldn't resist being swept up in the *what-if* scenario of it all. "And then you got the information about the Grid, the immersion packets, the implants—"

"Exactly," Hedges nodded. "We responded with our own scripted crystal and that's how we were able to open a line of communication between here and our relay hub. Since then, it's been easy to communicate back and forth."

With that, Hedges swiped his tablet and tapped on an icon labeled GRID RELAY.

Another hologram appeared in the center of the room. It was more compact, with what appeared to be main hubs connecting galaxy superclusters.

Oscar saw that one of the relays—near the Virgo supercluster—had a checkmark next to it.

Hedges pointed to the marked station. "This is our Grid hub. When I'm ready to send to—or receive from—the Grid, I request a messenger-Q."

Hedges tapped on a Q-MAIL icon. "The Grid responds by pinging an mQ near our collectors. The collectors only trap mQs with Earth's crypto key. They're held in an aerogel trap, waiting for our scripted data, which is THEN mirrored onto its twin at the nearest relay junction, then mirrored to another at the Grid library for retrieval ... or filing."

"When you send your messenger-Q, how does the Grid know it's a request from Earth, from this location?"

"Over billions of years, the Grid has tagged particles with distinct codes, codes they assign to each Grid member—each planet. The hub is pinged whenever one of our keys—our crypto signature—is sent out. It responds to the nearest entangled twin."

"Elegant." Oscar appreciated the simplicity of the design and thought, if it wasn't that way in reality, it should be.

"So, now that you've seen everything, do you have any thoughts on what happened on Saturday? Any idea how your experiment grabbed hold of the partial immersion packet? Back in the Ops Center, didn't you say something about a weakness in our q-state detection?"

Oscar nodded, "Yeah, can you pull up the schematic? Also, the program code you're using for qubit transfer...."

"Sure ... let's go sit down."

Hedges swiped his touchpad and the hologram disappeared. Now that it was empty, the Grid room seemed ten times larger. And colder, somehow.

Oscar followed Hedges to the right, into a side room. The room was similar to the Ops Center, but smaller: oval, with a desk and several chairs. Paper-thin displays lined the curved walls.

They sat and Hedges pulled up the q-state detection schematic and pointed it to the center display. Then, an adjacent display was filled with program code.

Oscar recognized some of the syntax, from the partial file his experiment had snagged. The complete code, the one currently onscreen, was much easier to understand, now that he was able to see the entire file and comments. "May I?"

Hedges handed the touchpad to Oscar, who scrolled through the code.

"This is for transferring the Cerulean packet from the Onculus back to QUINN?"

"Exactly."

Hedges was a clean coder and comments were sprinkled liberally throughout the program. Oscar knew what he was looking for and the weakness was easy to spot.

"There!" Oscar pointed to a line of code, near the bottom of the page. The data integrity command, the q-checksum set to run at the end of the program, was missing a hash switch. "That must be how my experiment was able to pick up the file, when the packet was retrieved from the brain and returned to QUINN. Somehow, on Saturday, those qubits were at the right place at the right time. Then, when I ran my experiment to find cryptographic signatures—BAM!—I got hold of your particles and they ended up in my ion trap."

Hedges peered at the code and slowly nodded. "You're right, man … there it is. How the hell did I miss *that*?"

Oscar handed the tablet back to Hedges, who edited the offending code. Then, he ran several tests; each time, there were no errors.

"I think we got it." Hedges sat back and smiled at Oscar, but his celebration was short-lived.

A voice came overhead, causing Hedges to jump and nearly drop the touchpad.

"So, you geniuses got 'er fixed?"

CHAPTER 50

Oscar looked at the COMM display and saw COMM: EB-II on the center of the screen.

Hedges regained his composure and said, "Yes, it looks like everything's operational."

"Well, ya told me that once before, but I guess I have no choice but to believe you this time."

Pause.

"I don't need to tell you what to do now, do I?"

"No, sir," Hedges said through clenched teeth.

When it was apparent Pierce had signed off, Oscar looked at Hedges, expecting to see Mr. Biggle had returned.

Sure enough, the guy had gone back into the dark place he went to whenever the Pantheon Director made an appearance—whether in voice or in person.

"Isn't there usually a *click*: a warning?" Oscar raised an eyebrow.

Now, it was clear why the guy was so on edge, and Oscar was more thankful than ever that he worked alone, with nobody else to answer to, nobody hovering over his shoulder.

Hedges shrugged. "Sometimes there's a *click*, sometimes not ... depends on the mood."

Damn, Oscar thought, that's pretty messed up; no wonder the guy was so jumpy. "Must take some getting used to...."

"I hardly notice anymore; it's surprising what you get used to."

That reminded Oscar of something he'd heard once, he wasn't sure where—perhaps in a psychology class. "Frog soup."

"Huh?"

"Actually, I think it's called 'boiling frog syndrome', or something. Basically, if you put a frog in boiling water, it'll jump out, but if you put it in cold water first, *then* turn up the heat, the change in temperature will be so slight—so gradual—the frogs won't realize they're boiling ... until it's too late."

Hedges looked at Oscar, his expression inscrutable, and Oscar thought he'd overstepped. He was just a visitor after all, and messing with a man's work family could be like messing with his real family. The employee could say shit about his employer, but nobody else could....

But then Hedges smiled. It was a sad little smile, a smile of resignation.

"Yeah, soup's done."

There was such a fatalistic tone in his voice, such a sense of defeat, Oscar wondered what was behind the moroseness. Obviously, based on Hedges's behavior in the presence of the Pantheon Director, Derrick Pierce was largely to blame.

As far as Oscar could tell, Hedges was in the dream job of any quantum engineer—apart from having to deal with an eccentric hover-boss.

There had been plenty of times Oscar had kicked himself for turning down the Pantheon job. Now that he was there with Hedges, now that he saw the simulation they were working on, he knew there was a good chance Hedges was sitting in the seat that could've been Oscar's.

So what did the guy have to be so depressed about? He had unfettered access to the most advanced physics technology—an ionospheric collector array blanketing the entire planet, for God's sake....

Oscar couldn't help thinking the guy—somewhere along the way—had lost sight of how lucky he was. Then, he remembered what Hedges had whispered earlier, outside the auditorium.

"Hey, what did you mean before ... when you said you needed my help?"

Hedges paled and glanced at the COMM display. He shook his head, the look of resignation gone. It had been replaced by a look of pure fear.

Oscar realized then that Hedges wasn't just jumpy—the guy was terrified. Of Pierce.

To keep Hedges from getting more agitated, Oscar dropped any further attempt at that line of inquiry. He smiled and shook his head slightly.

And Hedges seemed to relax when Oscar let it go.

CHAPTER 51

Finally, Pierce thought, things were getting back on track, but now, there was something new to worry about; he didn't like the way the kids were talking, and he knew Oscar Rand was the problem. It was what he'd been worried about, from the moment the kid had stepped into the lobby.

The kid's background file, the one Pierce had read during orientation, contained references to the usual bleeding-heart twaddle you'd hear about from kids too young and naïve to understand how the world really worked. Open-source activism, antitrust sit-ins, peace rallies. The poofy-haired kid made the rounds.

Damn fools seemed to think the machinery of progress ran under the power of unicorns and rainbows....

Even worse, Oscar was from old money—one of those spoiled brats who probably hadn't been taught the value of a hard day's work.

What other twenty-five-year-old, fresh out of school, could afford to turn down a seven-figure salary in favor of non-profit research?

Pierce's own parents may have been rich, but there had been no free lunches in his household. His father made him work in the oilfields, made him work as a worm on the lowest rung of the roughneck ladder—sometimes 20 hours a day—from the time he was able to climb a rig.

Bottom line was, Oscar was starting to ask a lot of useless questions and was becoming a distraction to Hedges. It was putting ideas into the kid's head, ideas that didn't need to be there.

Hedges could be a whiner at times, but at least he came from a hard-working, blue-collar background; kid respected money and knew that sometimes, things had to be done, things you might never think you'd do ... things that needed to be done for the greater good.

Pierce tugged at his shirt cuffs. Maybe it was a blessing that Oscar had turned down the job, back then. Now, the fact that Oscar had a few IQ points over on Hedges didn't seem so important....

Besides, the one thing that nerdlet could have brought to the table—the thing Hedges had used to create QUINN—Pierce got anyway.

He always got the intellectual property, directly or indirectly.

The poofy-haired kid thought it was all just a simulation, but just in case he started to stir up trouble, Pierce needed to be ready, so he commed security.

"Reggie, deliver that package to my office."

CHAPTER 52

Hedges was worried. Now that the system issues were resolved, things were moving quickly—too quickly. They had only a few hours before the tech library would be unlocked.

He'd hoped that, by now, Oscar would understand what was at stake. But Pierce had shut that down by telling Oscar it was all a simulation. And Pierce was always watching, always listening.

Hedges was surprised that Oscar was still there; Security hadn't been called in to take Oscar away.

Instead, they remained in the Edit Bay and Hedges put the finishing touches on Earth's immersion packet, all the while, he explained the process. He still hoped that, the more Oscar knew, the better the chance the entire operation would become real—too real to be a simulation.

"So, this is where I edit immersions," Hedges said, and opened the working copy of the packet.

Screenshots of the recorded scenes filled each of the displays, including the bungee scene in South Africa, the café in Paris, and the Autobahn scene.

"These were recorded from an implant? How is your sensory experience translated into something that can be played back by an exoplanetary brain? Brainmaps would be different throughout the Universe, right?"

"Right, it's all done with universal translators. Impulses fired from sensory input received by the visual and auditory processing systems are recorded and converted into a reproduction of the scene. The recordings are translated into qubits and *neural*bits, bundled into a packet, and messengered to the Grid. The Grid converts all new packets to be consistent with universal standards—so they may be played back on any implant. Add-ons are embedded into each new packet, including language translators and a library of trillions of different species' neural maps."

Oscar was quiet then, contemplating the images on the wall screens. Then he said, "Tell me again about the implant. All those people in the auditorium have agreed to have something injected in their thalamus? Seems like a hell of a lot of risk for a sim...."

Hedges nodded and pulled up a diagram of neural pathways. Lines and arrows started at the thalamic junction and branched out to show the path of afferent signals to different areas of the brain—to different processing layers throughout the cerebral cortex.

"It looks like a motherboard diagram," Oscar said.

"Exactly, but our brains are much more powerful—"

Oscar grinned. "Right ... but the singularity is near."

Hedges laughed. "Maybe, it's closer than you think."

Oscar raised an eyebrow, but Hedges continued with his explanation of immersion travel. "Anyway, the carbon-based implant is programmed to bond with the thalamic interneuron dendrites in the dorsal lateral geniculate nucleus ... programmed to trick the brain into treating it like any other interneuron. The implant becomes a new junction box in the relay station, a new signaling conductor."

"How does the Onculus communicate with the implant?"

"The packet information is sent via laser through the retina, through the optic tract, back to the thalamic region ... to the implant chip. The implant triggers the packet's neural firing sequences, immersing the user in the scene, just as the native recorder had been...."

"Who designed this?"

Hedges sighed and muttered. "Designed by *Them*, interpreted by us."

At Oscar's quizzical look, he continued, "A whole slew of people from all over the Ranch: consultants in neuroinformatics, neurobiology, biochemistry, genomics, user interface designers, and human computer interaction people. We got the blueprints from the Grid, translated the instructions for all system components, built the Onculus, and installed the PIT rooms. Each team only worked on part of each component, with none of the contractors knowing what the end product was."

"Puzzle projects...."

Hedges looked at Oscar and thought, *Dude sure blurts out some random shit.*

CHAPTER 53

Oscar was reminded of Teddy's description of puzzle projects and—as he listened to Hedges and looked at the neuroinformatics diagrams—he thought there was a good chance he was looking at some of her handiwork.

He dug in his pocket for his phone. "I gotta tell Teddy about this."

Hedges shook his head, looking grave. "You can't tell anyone."

"Why not? She probably already knows. Probably worked on some of this...." Oscar pointed his cell phone at the displays.

Hedges opened his mouth to speak, then glanced at the COMM display. "Sorry, we don't have time," he said. "I've got to get the flat version of this ready for Pierce's review. Besides, you won't get service down here."

Oscar shrugged and tucked his phone back in his pocket. It was worth a shot, but, given Pierce's intensity about not letting him run back to his lab—earlier in the day—and the reference to Teddy's security clearance, he knew it was a long shot.

No matter; he was now distracted by a new thought.

"Why wouldn't you just load the final packet into one of the PIT rooms?" He gestured toward one of the screens, the one showing the PIT room schedule.

At the moment, they could see the activity log for each room, as well as information about upcoming appointments. Including queued packet requests.

Hedges looked confused by the question. "What would Pierce do with an immersion?"

"He'd play the packet back—on his implant. Right? I mean, isn't that what the rooms are for?"

"Yeah, but *Pierce* wouldn't—," Hedges started to say, his brow furrowed, then his confusion cleared. "Oh, yeah! You don't know about that, do you? Pierce can't do trips, not anymore."

"Why not?"

"It happened during early testing," Hedges replied, and, with another furtive glance at the COMM display, said no more on the subject.

CHAPTER 54

Pierce tugged at his shirt cuffs and his footsteps lightened when he saw the number of occupied PIT rooms. He read the names as they scrolled across the signs.

In session were Prince Henri, Hans Kurzweil, and Prime Minister Gordon Landham, among others; the new users had wasted no time in scheduling their maiden voyages.

But, one name was not on any of the signs: Senator Higgs. He hoped ol' Wally hadn't wimped out.

He veered toward the Ops Center, went in, and sat down. The COMM locator showed that the kids were still in the Edit Bay, working on the review packet. He didn't want to break in on that; the nerdlets were slow enough as it was.

He pulled up the PIT user interface and frowned at the cursor blinking in the password field. Realizing he'd have to interrupt anyway, he commed the Edit Bay. "What's my password?"

Pierce typed it in as the kid rattled it off. He reached out to flip off the COMM but then, decided to leave it on—with the sound and video set to 1-way.

Once he was logged into the PIT user system, Pierce clicked on the SCHEDULE icon and scrolled through the list of user activity. He smiled when he finally saw what he was looking for.

Wally was in PIT-13. In fact, according to the room log, his trip was well underway.

Very fine ... all going like clockwork now.

He sat back and watched the Edit Bay feed; it looked like the kid was editing the Autobahn scene, which—if he was going in recording order—meant it was almost done.

After all his hard work, after all the time and money he'd spent on QUINN and the PIT, it was finally—

Pierce's celebration was cut short when an alarm sounded.

BWAWWWNK! BWAWWWNK! BWAWWWNK!

The deep bass of the alarm drilled into Pierce's head and strobe lights pulsed up and down the hallways. It was as if the Pantheon underground had been transformed into a bomb shelter. One in the middle of an emergency drill.

BWAWWWNK! BWAWWWNK! BWAWWWNK!

Pierce saw Doc Thompson rush out of his office and into the hallway. He sprinted toward one of the PIT rooms.

The light over PIT-13—the Senator's room—was blinking red, blue, and yellow, like the flashing lights of a cop car. Thompson stopped when he reached the door and yanked it open.

Pierce ran out and shouted, "What the hell's going on?!"

Doc Thompson yelled back, "Senator Higgs flatlined!" Then, he disappeared into the room.

CHAPTER 55

BWAWWWNK! BWAWWWNK! BWAWWWNK!

While the Doc tended to Wally in PIT-13, Pierce rushed to the Ops Center to turn off the alarm and flashing lights. He swiped at the security console, at the COMM controls, until he finally hit the right icons.

The alarm went silent and the lights stopped flashing.

In Pierce's haste to silence the alarm, he accidentally flipped 2-way on the COMM feed, which was pointed at the Edit Bay—pointed at Oscar and Hedges.

Pierce didn't notice.

He was worried the rest of the users would panic, would think that immersion travel wasn't safe. So worried, they might feel compelled to tell someone on the outside....

It wasn't the users in the PIT rooms he was worried about—they wouldn't hear a peep while in immersion. He *was* concerned, however, about the few stragglers hanging out in the halls.

Thankfully, Reggie and the rest of the security detail managed to calm everyone down. They were told Wally was being treated for jet lag from his

Geneva trip, and there was nothing to worry about—*nothing to see here.*

It was true enough, Pierce thought. *They* probably didn't need to worry. *Their* brain scans had been cleared with no issues.

The Doc stood outside PIT-13 and watched as the Senator's gurney was wheeled away. Pierce caught his eye and waved him over.

Thompson joined him, his expression grim. "He's dead. We killed him! I told you his brain couldn't handle immersions," he said, wringing his hands and pacing the Ops Center.

Neither noticed the open Edit Bay COMM.

Pierce snorted, "It's your fault ... your neuro gadgets—"

"It's *not* the Onculus. It's *not* the implants!"

"Just go dissolve the implant and make sure the coroner's report reads right."

"And if I refuse?"

Pierce shrugged. "I suppose you *could,* but isn't the implant *your* smoking gun, not mine? Relax ... we get the tech library this afternoon, remember? And after those nerdlets finish up our packet, it'll all be over but the cryin'."

"What does *that* mean?"

"I'm thinkin' I'll shut the whole thing down. I'll have the secrets of the Universe; I won't need any of you anymore. Not you. Not the rest of the nerdlets."

Pierce sneered at Thompson, pulled out a cigar, and made a production of clipping the end and lighting it.

Thompson shook his head, looking incredulous. "Do you honestly think these people, these world leaders, are gonna go away quietly and let you control the tech—whatever you find?"

"They don't know about the tech, remember?"

"Even so, they won't take too kindly to you shutting down Grid access. No matter how much power you think you have over these people, a discovery of this magnitude can't be kept quiet for much longer; there are already rumors—"

"There are *always* rumors about Pantheon. No matter, tomorrow, PIT operations will be shut down and the beta testers will be told it was all a simulation."

"Oh, come on; who's gonna believe that?"

"I just told the smartest person at Agrippa and he had no trouble chokin' it down."

That shut the Doc up, at least for a moment. Then he started up again.

"You're forgetting about me and Hedges. At least the two of us know everything—"

"Yeah, but you know better than to blab. You're not exactly innocent. You'll do well to remember that Marvin would still be alive and kickin' if you hadn't given him those pills. And the Senator would still be around if you hadn't given him the implant. Not to mention your role in the early trials, back by the barracks. No, my friend, if you think yer gonna run your mouth, remember that as far as anyone will know, you'll be just another mad scientist, just some frankendoctor down here, doing crazy whoozits without my knowledge. You might want to think about *that* before you decide to get all goody-goody on me."

"You said you'd never mention the early trials...."

Pierce shrugged and ignored the Doc's whining. "Yep, I believe it's time to shut 'er down, soon as the kid's done."

He started to turn toward the Edit Bay COMM, to check up on the kids, to check in on their progress. He was done with the Doc.

CHAPTER 56

In the Edit Bay, Hedges and Oscar sat in stunned silence, staring at the Ops Center feed.

Hedges knew he should turn it off, should turn it off before Pierce or Dr. Thompson noticed the open COMM, but he was paralyzed.

He watched as the Doc stormed out of the Ops Center. Then, Pierce turned. To Hedges, it was like watching him turn around in slow motion. But finally, Pierce saw....

He saw them watching, mouths agape, their horrified expressions saying it all—that they'd heard everything.

Hedges and Oscar flinched back in their chairs.

Pierce smiled, a cold smile, and his eyes narrowed. His face filled the frame—so close, Hedges could see the beginnings of the Director's five o'clock shadow.

It's getting late, Hedges thought, his mind skittering in all directions, not knowing what alarming thing to focus on.

He knew Pierce was crazy, had plans to jeopardize Earth's Grid access, but what Pierce and the Doc were talking about was murder. The murders of Senator Higgs and Marvin Trimble. And what was that about early trials ... in the barracks?

Hedges flashed on the image of the unfinished PIT rooms and the chairs with restraints—

"Kid, since ya got time to stick your nose where it don't belong, it must mean the packet's ready?"

Hedges could only manage to shake his head. He would have thought Pierce would be angry that he and Oscar had overheard the conversation, but he seemed calm. And that was much worse.

Click.

The two of them sat in silence for a while longer, still in shock.

Oscar was the first to speak. He looked pale. Shaken. "So, he lied ... it's not a simulation?"

"No. I'm sorry, I wanted to tell you. He's fuckin' nuts. He has me locked up down here—"

Oscar opened his mouth to speak, but it was too late. They heard the clomping of cowboy boots in the Grid room and cigar smoke wafted into the Edit Bay.

CHAPTER 57

"Why does everything have to be such a goddamn production?!"

They heard Pierce all the way across the expanse of the Grid room and through the Edit Bay door, his voice getting louder until he stood inside the room, glowering.

"If you spent more time workin' and less time spyin', you might be done by now."

Hedges realized that the time for a stealth plan—the time for coming up with some way to sneak word out about the Grid—that time was over. By Pierce's own admission, he planned on shutting everything down as soon as he got the tech.

Having never pushed back against his boss, he wasn't sure he could go through with it, but he took a deep breath and stood and faced the Pantheon Director. "What incentive do I have to finish this? Now that I know you plan on shutting everything down?"

Pierce's eyes narrowed and he advanced farther into the room. "We already went over this. I don't give two shits about Earth's Grid access. All I want is that damn tech library. You're too

187

naïve to understand, but open-sharing is a fool's dream. The Grid founders obviously don't know what idiots we got down here."

Hedges snorted. "You can't honestly believe you know better than civilizations billions of years more advanced? You think this is the first time the Grid has encountered beings like us?"

"You callin' me stupid?"

As usual, Pierce missed the point. He only heard his intelligence being questioned.

Pierce moved closer to Hedges. "Who the hell do you think you are? Without me, there'd be none of this," He waved his cigar around the Edit Bay and out toward the Grid room. "Ya think the quantum hoohah fairy came in one night and filled these rooms with all your toys? Don't go thinkin' just cuz I let you play with all this, you're in charge. *I'm* the one. *I'll* be the one in the record books."

Hedges laughed. "Oh really? You think *you're* going to be known as the inventor and founder of the Grid tech? Who's going to believe that? Everybody knows you're just the money guy. You're just another William Orton."

"Who?"

Hedges nodded, "You get my point: the guy who hired Edison and bankrolled his work. Everyone knows Edison's name, but where's Orton in the public's consciousness? I challenge you to find his name anywhere in the record books, except maybe in eight-point font in a footnote in a dusty volume of *Encyclopedia*

Britannica. Nobody ever remembers the money guy."

"Yeah? Well, apparently, *you* do," Pierce smirked.

"Fine ... anyone with an *idiotic* memory will remember your role in this. Without my brain—wait, no—," Hedges turned and pointed to Oscar, who was standing against a far wall. "Without *Oscar's* and my brain, you'd have never found the Grid. Without his q-state detection thesis, without the QUINN design and programming, none of this would have been created. No beacon would've been found—"

Pierce jabbed his finger into Hedges's chest. "Listen kid, it may be true your new butt-buddy here wrote a paper and you typed out some computer code, but chances are, some other nerd along the way would've done the same thing. And, dollars to donuts, I would've been right there, bankrolling *that* nerdlet, instead o' you. Do you know how many billions I've flushed down the toilet in the name of research? You brainiacs have been drainin' me dry for years. You're a bunch o' leeches is what ya are—starin' at your navels and scribblin' your doodles on whiteboards. So, yeah, of course I used your brain. I *own* it and anything it dreams up."

Pierce's Texas roots were showing, his drawl becoming thicker the more he ranted.

In the center of the Edit Bay, he and Hedges stood, toe-to-toe, breathing heavy, squared off like a couple of bulls. Neither backing down.

CHAPTER 58

Pierce looked at his watch. One forty-five.

The kids were burning precious time with the twaddle about not finishing the packet; he wished he could just boot 'em out and bring in some other nerds to finish the job.....

But training someone new would be even more of a time-killer, so he tried to diffuse the situation. "Look, let's all take a breather and relax ... just go ahead and queue up the review file so we can get on with it."

"I will ... on one condition," Hedges said, chin jutted forward, hands on his hips.

Oh for fuck's sake. "Are you sure you're in any position to set terms?"

"You still need my *freak brain* don't you? Or would you like to finish the uploading process yourself? Feeling up to doing qubit and *n*bit conversions, are ya?"

Pierce knew the kid thought he was stupid; how hard could it be to press a few buttons? It wasn't that he *couldn't* do it, he just had other things to worry about. He decided to humor the kid for a minute longer. "Whatdya want?"

"Make sure Grid access is free and available to all, including the tech library—as the founders intended."

Pierce snorted. "Impossible." These idiots thought the true gold of the Grid was in immersions, which only showed their lack of vision. As far as Pierce was concerned, they could blow the whole complex up ... ten billion years of inventions and tech was going to be more than enough for him. Unfortunately, the kid wasn't done harpin'.

"Everyone should know about this discovery, about the tech library ... you don't *own* the Universe, you know ... nobody does, that's the whole point of the co-op. If the Gridmaster cuts Earth off, there's no going back. We'll never get another chance ... Earth will never be issued another encryption key...."

"Believe me, it's for the best ... that whole open sharing concept is hogwash; the Grid's obviously not acquainted with the likes of humans. The moment the masses are allowed access, well, that'll be the end of it. Just look at Wally...."

"*You* did that to Senator Higgs."

"Whatever. What's done is done. So what? So now you know ... it's my choice to do whatever I want with my own property."

But the kid kept at it, "It should be free to all. It should be a right. It's how the Grid founders designed it; those are the rules we agreed to."

Pierce tugged at his cuffs, "Oh really, and who should be the one to fund all that free access?"

"You know it's wouldn't be that expensive. Building up PIT infrastructure all over the world would be easy, and the cost-per-trip would be less than the price of a latte. You said yourself that developing personal immersion devices would be as easy as modding any Pantheon tablet."

Pierce shook his head. "I'm sorry ... no. End of discussion. Now, load it up."

But the kid was proving to be more stubborn than Pierce thought.

"I don't think you have much of a choice."

CHAPTER 59

Oscar watched as Hedges stood up to the Pantheon Director and he wondered where Mr. Biggle had gone; at the moment, there was no sign of the fraidy-cat.

As the two squared off, Oscar tried to process everything he'd seen and heard. It wasn't a simulation after all. There really *were* beacons from an alien network. There really *was* an entire cooperative of shared experiences and knowledge going on throughout the Universe.

And foremost in his mind, was the realization that Pierce seemed hell-bent on ruining it for the rest of the planet.

Now that Oscar had a small glimpse of the Grid, even though he hadn't been able to experience an immersion, he knew he couldn't live in a world without such access—couldn't live in a world out in the cold, shunned from the rest of the Universe, knowing what there was out there … just out of reach.

Inspired by Hedges's display of courage, Oscar grabbed a tablet off the desk and swiped at its screen. He held the tablet up, with his finger on the delete button.

"If you don't send a live message out to the world right now—a message about the truth of the Grid—I'll delete the file containing Earth's immersion packet, every frame, every bit of it. Hedges tells me it's the only copy. After all, not submitting the packet will result in the same thing, right? Earth being locked out? The only difference is, you won't get your greedy hands on the tech..."

Pierce shot a look of pure venom at Oscar. He moved away from Hedges and advanced toward Oscar. "I knew it was a bad idea to let you in. Is this any way for a guest to behave? Did your parents teach you nothing? Now, hand over the tablet."

Oscar stepped back and shielded the tablet. He wondered if Pierce could tell he was bluffing. He could no sooner jeopardize the Grid connection than Hedges could, but could Pierce sense that?

Pierce studied Oscar and Hedges, then glanced at his watch.

For a moment, it seemed they might have won, but then Pierce smiled a chilling smile. The look did nothing to help smooth Oscar's nerves, which had been frayed ever since he'd walked into the Pantheon lobby.

He knew now that Pierce wasn't just some "Crazy Cowboy", some amusingly eccentric billionaire. He also finally knew why Hedges was so jumpy.

And, he was again reminded of the news clip from the other day, about sociopaths in business, in positions of power, and realized he was looking at a prime example.

Pierce made a show of going to the COMM controls, all the while, he smiled his cold smile.

"There's something in my office I think you boys should see."

The display flickered on and COMM: DPIERCE appeared.

He tapped until he found the camera angle he wanted and an image filled the screen.

Now, they could see an old gun in a velvet lined box, sitting atop a pedestal, as in a museum display.

"So?" Hedges said, unimpressed. "It's just your ratty old pistol."

CHAPTER 60

Oscar assumed Pierce was threatening them with the gun. An object out of reach—up in the Director's office—and he snickered. "Not a lotta help that pistol's gonna be, unless you plan on beaming it down."

Pierce, who had calmed considerably, smiled and said, "It's a revolver, actually. And no, I'm not gonna 'beam it down'; Hedges tells me that ain't possible ... now, whether or not that's true, I won't know til later, will I? That is, if you kids stop screwin' around and let me get my tech library."

"Anyway," he continued. "There *is* a pistol in my office ... a whole nuther kind, if that's what you're into." He looked at Oscar. "And, I think you might be *very* into this one." Pierce reached over and tapped on UNMUTE. "Say hello, kitten," he drawled and stood back—waiting.

First, there was only her voice. "Hey, numbnuts! Is this the coolest thing or what?"

Then, Teddy bounded into frame and pulled the gun out of the case. She waved it in the air, then aimed it, like she was Annie Oakley and Pierce's office was the Wild West.

Gutpunched, Oscar lost all feeling in his legs. He stumbled back and dropped into a chair. He lost his grip on the tablet and it crashed to the floor. He didn't notice, he could only stare at the display, at Teddy, and his head began to buzz.

My Teddy? In the crazy fuck's office. She has no idea what's going on. Has no idea she's in danger. And it's all my fault! If I hadn't called her about the file....

Without thinking, he shot out of the chair and lunged at Pierce. He was fueled by panic, by fear, by rage. He flailed at the larger man with his fists and, at the same time, yelled at the display, "TEDDY, RU—"

But Pierce was fast.

He grabbed Oscar, flipped him around against his chest, and clamped a hand over his mouth.

The smell of stale cigars filled Oscar's nostrils and he gagged. His mind was dragged back to the house in Boston, back to long-buried thoughts of his stepfather—the cigars, the beer, the rec room....

He felt hot breath on his ear as Pierce whispered, "Kid ... you'd better think carefully about your next move."

The fight drained from Oscar's body when he realized Pierce had the upper hand, but panic remained.

Pierce pulled his hand away and shoved Oscar to the side, shooting him a look of warning.

"Oscar?" High above, Teddy's smile faded and she glanced around Pierce's office. She held the gun loosely now, her arms hung by her sides.

She looked confused.

Oscar's heart contracted and his stomach twisted into knots; obviously, the video was set to 1-way.

Teddy, what the hell are you doing here?! RUN!! This guy's a l-u-n-a-t-i-c!

"Kid, aren't you gonna answer your friend? It ain't polite to keep a lady waiting, especially one as fine as our kitten."

Teddy tilted her head and her smile slowly returned, "Yeah, don't keep me hangin'," she said and put one hand on her hip while waving the other, the one with the gun, in the air. "I got a gun, you know," she teased.

Oscar ferreted around in his mind for one of those brilliant super-secret, insider-only coded messages to feed to Teddy; to clue her in on the danger of the situation, but his brain had chosen that moment to take a break ... *a little afternoon siesta, perhaps?*

Thanks a lot, guy. You're great in the shower, but on dry land, when it truly matters, hoooboy! You're 'bout as useless as a ... as a ... boat. Hah! Nice one, Genius. Way to round that out ... creative. Firing on all cylinders ain'tcha? Snappy dappy pappy—

SHUT IT!

There would be no super-secret message. Feeling queasy, he was only able to manage a weak: "Hey, jerkytits, whatchya doin' here?"

CHAPTER 61

Teddy perked up when she heard Oscar's voice.

She sauntered around the office—breezy, carefree—and said, "Well, I was minding my own business over at Neuropath, about to go and get you for lunch, as a matter of fact—to find out what the heck all that was about earlier ... when some Pantheon guys came to my office—you know, all covert ops and shit—and they told me you needed my help. I figured it had something to do with that video game file. Amiright? Where are you and Mr. Pierce, anyway?" Again, she glanced around the office.

"C'mon now, kitten, I asked you to call me Derrick," Pierce drawled, and shot another look of warning at Oscar, who'd instinctively made a move forward. Then he said, "Hang on; I'll be up in a minute."

Pierce swiped at the COMM controls and the feed went blank. He turned to Oscar and Hedges and folded his arms over his chest. He smiled, clearly enjoying himself.

Now that Teddy couldn't hear, Oscar lunged at Pierce, "You crazy sonuvabitch, if you hurt her, I'll kill you!"

Pierce side-stepped the attack and kept Oscar at arm's length.

For a moment, they stood there and Oscar tried to catch his breath. Tried to understand what was going on. He stared at the blank COMM display, feeling helpless.

Pierce smiled and said, "Look, I don't want to do anything to your friend; but I need to protect my interests. You needed to know I'll do whatever it takes to ensure the tech library gets into the right hands." He grabbed Oscar's arm and started toward the door. Over his shoulder he said, "Get my file done."

CHAPTER 62

After Pierce led Oscar out, Hedges sat, confused and disoriented, his cotton-head had returned. Maybe, it had never left.

For a brief moment, when Oscar had stepped in and threatened Pierce with destroying the packet—their key to the tech library—Hedges thought it was what he'd been waiting for. It would have been brilliant, if only Pierce hadn't been one step ahead, ready with his insurance.

Now, all they'd succeeded in doing was to send Pierce into a higher level of crazy, and yet *another* person was at risk.

Hedges knew Pierce wouldn't simply let Oscar and Teddy free. He wouldn't just release them back out into the Ranch—out into the world—free to tell everyone what was going on.

He looked at the clock. There was little more than an hour before the deadline and he briefly considered what would happen if he refused to finish. Pierce admitted his plan was to shut down the Grid, so trying to preserve Earth's access seemed to be moot.

But, no, he couldn't give up. Not while there was still time.

He couldn't do anything about Oscar, but he *could* keep an eye on him.

Hoping Pierce wasn't watching, he picked up the tablet, and slid it onto his lap. Keeping it partly shielded by the desk, he opened the security interface.

He ran a search for unauthorized pheromone signatures in the building, knowing he should see two ... no ... *three* signatures: his own—since his access had been deactivated on Friday—and the signatures of Oscar and Teddy.

Now, the screen displayed a map of the building, with several dozen green dots pinpointing the locations of recognized pheromone signatures. And, as he'd hoped, there were three red dots showing the signatures not in the database.

As long as the signatures remained in the building, as long as they were detected, at least he'd know they were alive.

Keeping one eye on the tablet, Hedges moved forward with finishing the review packet for Pierce. All the while, his mind searched for a plan.

Now that Oscar was gone, it would be up to him to save the Grid access, the tech library, and maybe—their lives.

CHAPTER 63

Oscar thought they were headed to the sideways elevator. He thought Pierce was taking him to his office, to see Teddy. Instead, they stopped when they were halfway down the hall.

Pierce opened one of the PIT room doors and commanded, "Sit down."

Oscar walked in and looked around, hoping to see Teddy, knowing he wouldn't.

It was a small room with a chair, an Onculus—like the one on stage in the auditorium—and a wall display. Next to the chair was a tablet control.

Other than that, the room was empty.

"Where's Teddy?"

Pierce ignored the question. "One of my hobbies, when I'm not helping nerdlets with their inventions, is rare game hunting. Ever tried that?"

"Fuck you. Take me to Teddy."

Pierce ignored him, walked over to the chair, and picked up the tablet. "It's incredible. There's a hunting ground in South Africa very few people know about. When the kid and I were there for our recording tour, I took a little side trip and got myself a new prize. Anyway, here ya go, kid—a tiger for a kitten," Pierce swiped at the tablet, and an image appeared on the wall display.

At the sight of the video, Oscar's face drained of all color. He read the message under the video feed and stumbled to the chair, sat down and stared at the display. "I'll do whatever you want ... just don't hurt her. *Please.*"

"Play nice and you'll find I'm a reasonable guy," Pierce said. "Once you've had the chance to reflect, you'll realize it's in your—and your girlfriend's—best interest to keep your attitude in check. It ain't helping your new buddy Hedges, and it sure as shit ain't good for your girl." He pivoted on a boot heel and started toward the door, then he turned back and said, "If you get out of that chair, I'll know ... and my new prize will get some catnip."

CHAPTER 64

Pierce zoomed up to his office and wondered how things had gone to shit so far, so fast.

The system alert on Saturday had been the start of the downhill slide, and now, the Senator Higgs thing had made it snowball.

It was too bad the kids had overheard his conversation with the Doc, but no matter, at least he'd had the good sense to bring the girl in; once again, his insurance paid off.

Pierce dreaded the thought of the cleanup ... later on. There was Hedges, Oscar, and the girl ... even ol' Doc Thompson was showing signs he might not be up to the end game, may not be able to bring it across the finish line. It would be tricky to maneuver through all the loose ends and bruised egos, but, he'd dealt with egos far bigger in the past and still managed to come out on top....

One thing Pierce was happy about was his brilliant inspiration to tell everyone it was a sim; it would be the perfect way to get a clean break from his "beta testers", and, as a bonus, he could turn the whole Grid operation into an app to end all apps—

The elevator stopped and he glanced at the tablet in his hand. Calm had been restored; Hedges was working in the Edit Bay and Oscar was in the PIT room. It was much better now that they were separated.

He had to keep the poofy-haired kid and the girl there; it would give Hedges more incentive to stay on track, besides, one—or all—of their freak brains might come in handy.

Pierce exited the elevator, tugged at his shirt cuffs, and headed toward his office. Through the open door, he saw the girl. She was standing by the windows and he joined her.

He looked out over Agrippa, at his domain. It was mid-afternoon and the food trucks were gone. The helipad was empty.

By then, Higgs's body would have been airlifted back to D.C., where the coroner's report would read: ruptured aneurism, caused by air travel. The medical examiner owed him one.

He looked at the girl, smiled and said, "Sorry for keeping you waiting and for all the secrecy; it's just that your friend's helping us out with a little something ... if you wouldn't mind hanging around for a while, I may or may not have something for you to consult on."

He sat down and commed Doc Thompson.

She smiled, shrugged, pranced over to the desk and sat down.

"Doc, I trust the package is safely on its way?"

"Yes, sir."

The girl looked at the display. "Hey, is that—"

Oh for fuck's sake! Pierce had enough of nerdlets interrupting him all day. He looked over at the girl and said, "Pipe down!"

"Pipe d— *Excuse* you?"

She arched her eyebrows to the sky and sat back, arms folded, her pretty little lips fixed in a straight line. She wasn't happy, but, at least she'd shut her pie-hole.

CHAPTER 65

Teddy fumed. Until then, she'd enjoyed the adventure and mystery of the day; it beat looking at stacks of fMRI scans and program code.

When she was brought to Pantheon, to the Crazy Cowboy's office, she'd been curious to see inside, and even more curious to see what Oscar was helping them with. Not to mention, it was pretty cool to ride in a sideways elevator....

At first, she'd been flattered by Pierce's flirtation; she'd had a thing for cowboys back in the day. True, it had faded as she got older, but remnants of the early obsession remained. So, yeah, she hadn't minded the mild flirtation; he was a good looking older man—mysterious. A bad boy.

But now, as she looked across the desk and saw him sitting back in his chair, chomping on a stinky cigar, with his cowboy boots propped up, she felt ill.

She flashed to earlier in the day ... when she had discovered that her office and lab were wired. *So creepy.* And ... she wasn't accustomed to being shushed. *Pipe down?! Really?*

No. The arrogant, dismissive type was definitely *not* her thing.

Her thoughts turned to Oscar then. Sweet Oscar with his quirks, his wild hair, and his complete lack of artifice. He thought logically and had a difficult time with some nuances of speech—like sarcasm—but Teddy saw that as a good thing. Would she really want to him to be snarky, to learn how to put on an affect, to be just like all the other asshats of the world? No way.

One thing was certain; the shine was quickly fading on the afternoon's adventure.

She just wanted to see Oscar, wherever he was. It was nifty and all, being invited to the inner sanctum—was cool to see the Colt revolver that reminded her of Civil War reenactments, like the ones Oscar drug her to.

Thinking of those times helped to take the edge off her irritation. Sure, she grumbled whenever he turned up with tickets to those things, but—if she were honest with herself—she'd have to admit how much she looked forward to those times.

She half-listened to the conversation between the Pantheon Director and Dr. Neil Thompson, a man she'd instantly recognized as a well-respected pioneer in neuroinformatics and human computer interaction. A man with about a gazillion published articles—

Just then, Pierce kicked his feet off the desk and, in the process, a pad of paper shifted over and uncovered a tablet.

What Teddy saw on the tablet's screen made her blood run cold and, for a moment, her heart stopped.

It was Oscar! And he sat, frozen in terror, looking across a room at a snarling tiger.

CHAPTER 66

Teddy's mind raced. She had to get out of there; she had to find Oscar.

She looked across the desk at Pierce, and realized—for the first time since entering the building—she was in danger.

Had he noticed her face was pale, that her hands were shaking? It was all she could do to keep from running from the room, to keep from tearing through the building to find her friend.

She stood and tried to look calm, slightly bored, like it was just any other day, hanging out in an office with the most powerful man in the world.

With one eye on Pierce, who was still engrossed in his conversation with Thompson, Teddy slowly walked past the gun display.

She could grab the gun ... then what? Was she going to shoot Pierce right there, in his own office?

She decided to wait for a chance to run for the elevators. From there, she didn't know what she'd do, but she couldn't just sit around.

Her chance came when Pierce ended his conversation and cleared the COMM screen.

He stood and said, "Be right back" and disappeared through a side door. Before he shut the door behind him, she saw a marble vanity. A bathroom.

Teddy sprang into action.

She rushed over to the display, grabbed the gun, and dropped it into her oversized pocket, then, she dashed out of the room. Her heart crashed against her chest and blood thumped in her ears. She ran to the elevator and searched for the call button. Not finding one, not seeing any card access, she waved her arms and paced back and forth.

She became frantic; any moment Pierce would notice she was gone. She stared at the bank of unresponsive elevators.

How the hell do these doors open?!

Then, from the office doorway, she heard his voice ... that *creepy-crawly* drawl, "Works on sensors—pheromones. It won't recognize yours, I'm afraid."

Pierce leaned against the door jamb with an amused expression on his face.

Teddy's fingertips tingled and her legs felt like rubber. She backed away toward the last elevator, near the far wall, and thrust her hands into her pockets. She was emboldened by the solid feel of the revolver. "Take me to Oscar, now!"

"Sorry, kitten, no can do; you'll be more useful to me up here."

He moved toward her, still smiling, looking like he was enjoying himself. He looked down at her pocket and smiled wider.

Of course, she thought, he would have noticed the empty case when he came out of the bathroom.

So why was the crazy fuck so calm?

Pierce continued to advance—

Ding!

Teddy was startled when the elevator doors closest to her opened.

She ran into the elevator and reached for the floor selection buttons. But the wall was bare. Her heart sank when she remembered her ride up. The security guard had used—

"Voice commands," Pierce said. "Sorry, did I forget to mention that?" He shrugged. "It's amazing, really, the things you nerdlets come up with. When you're not whinin', that is. Without you, I guess we'd still be punchin' buttons or swipin' cards. Shit, climbin' stairs, for that matter...."

He was nonchalant. Without a care in the world.

Teddy stood in the middle of the useless elevator, dazed. Finally, she snapped out of it.

She yanked the Colt out of her pocket and pointed it at him, praying she looked more intimidating than she felt.

"*This* doesn't need a voice command," She said and steadied the gun, aiming it at his chest.

214

Pierce laughed. "No, kitten, that's true ... but last I checked, it *does* need bullets. C'mon; you don't think I'd leave a loaded gun in a room with some filly, do ya?"

Still chuckling, he turned and headed back to his office. Over his shoulder he said, "Now, come on back ... I got shit to do and you're wastin' time."

For a moment, Teddy just stood there, feeling sick. Then, she charged out of the elevator. She ran, full throttle, at Pierce's retreating back.

He was already in the office, nearly at his desk, when he finally heard her and he whipped around—a little too late.

She whacked him on the side of his head, hard, with the butt of the gun.

Pierce looked surprised and stumbled backward, back against the desk. Teddy stood—shaking, her arm still raised, the gun still clutched in her hand. She watched, horrified, as blood began to seep into the gash over his temple.

She was surprised by her own violence, by her rage, and when she saw the pain in the Director's eyes, she felt a twinge of guilt. But that emotion would be short-lived.

In a flash, the pain in his eyes was replaced by something else. Enjoyment.

CHAPTER 67

Pierce looked at the girl. Her shoulder strap had come undone and the tank top underneath was torn. Scraps of red lace and ribbon peeked out.

"Well, well; looks like little kitten's hiding a tiger inside." Fitting, he thought.

"Take me to Oscar!" She screamed and again charged forward.

But Pierce was ready this time. He reached out and pressed his palm against her forehead, holding her at arm's length, to stop her from doing any more damage.

For a little thing, she sure was feisty. At any other time, he might have enjoyed their little dance, but he didn't have time to horse around.

He pushed her, hard, and she flew back toward the gun display. Her head hit the corner of the pedestal with a satisfying *THUNK,* and she crumpled to the floor.

He reached up and pressed his fingers to the cut on the side of his head, felt the hot, sticky blood, and pulled his hand back.

Bitch bled me....

He commed security. "Reggie, get up here."

By the time Reggie arrived at the office, Pierce was on his way back down to the PITs.

CHAPTER 68

Oscar sat frozen, unable to tear his eyes from the video feed. On the display, he saw a room, divided by a heavy, wrought iron wall—as if in a medieval dungeon. On one side, a tiger paced and snarled.

The tiger's muscles rippled underneath its striped pelt. It would get close to the bars, would crouch and snarl at the empty chair on the other side, then it would resume pacing. Snarl and pace … rinse and repeat.

Oscar looked at the empty chair on the other side of the wall. The message under the chair chilled his blood.

RESERVED FOR KITTEN

It's my fault.

If he hadn't brought her into this mess, hadn't shown her the partial Pantheon file, hadn't mentioned her name to Pierce … she'd still be safe, back in her lab, swaying to Bob Marley and looking at brain scans.

How could I have been so careless?

Oscar suddenly felt like Hedges looked: terrified, confused, exhausted.

He had whiplash from the things he'd seen and heard over the past few hours. First, Pierce told him about an alien internet, then he told him it was all a sim, and now he said it wasn't a sim, and he intended to shut it all down.

Frankly, Oscar wasn't sure what to think about the whole Grid thing—about the Onculus and the immersion packets.

An alien net and some ten billion years of tech seemed such a remote, abstract concept, it paled in comparison to seeing the most important person in his life being threatened.

His world had been reduced to a snarling tiger and an empty chair.

Aware that Pierce might be watching, he surreptitiously swiped the tablet. Keeping an eye on the tiger feed, he rooted around the tablet's directory for anything he could use.

To use for what, he wasn't sure....

After opening icons and seeing only login screens, he discovered the only thing he had—without logging in—was limited access to the PIT room schedule.

He knew Hedges always had an eye on the schedule in order to monitor PIT activity, and he wondered if there was a way he could use that knowledge ... there must be *something* he could do, but it had to be quick.

If Pierce got what he wanted, the time for plans would be over.

CHAPTER 69

Branson Ross sat in the auditorium and half-listened as his peers gossiped about the Walter Higgs incident.

After orientation, Branson had left Pantheon for another meeting at Agrippa and, upon his return, learned about the Senator's ruptured aneurysm.

The others told Branson it was caused by air travel, from the flight back from Geneva, but Branson had concerns, and not just about the safety of immersion travel.

At first—back when Derrick Pierce approached him with a fantastic tale of an alien internet and planet immersions—he'd written it off as another of Pierce's pranks. When Pierce finally convinced him to go to the underground and see the Grid, Branson reluctantly signed up for the beta test, if only to keep an eye on the operation.

He didn't trust Pierce. If Branson saw any signs of withholding access or abusing Grid privileges in any way, he was ready to take action. Pierce had powerful friends, but Branson had just as many, just as powerful, and he wasn't about to let the Crazy Cowboy ruin it for the rest of the world.

Upon hearing the news about Higgs, Branson talked to Doc Thompson, who assured him immersion travel was safe, assured him that the Senator's death had been an isolated, unrelated incident. He trusted and respected Thompson, having worked with him in the past, so Branson decided to forge ahead.

Now, he sat and browsed through the packet selection menus and, although Earth was restricted to a fraction of the Grid library, there were still many options to consider.

He narrowed the selection by filtering the extrasensory options, then checked his suggestion queue.

In the end, he chose a planet that had been preselected for him—one tagged because his brainmap indicated somatosensory preferences similar to those of another species, on another planet....

According to one review, SPIDER 84a was: "A conflict free world, its inhabitants capable of interspecies communication." Sounded more than fine to Branson, who'd often tried to imagine what a peaceful world would be like.

His choice made, Branson tapped on RESERVE, and a message appeared.

RESERVATION CONFIRMED
B. ROSS: PIT-1>> SPIDER 84a >> 3:00 P.M.

CHAPTER 70

Oscar couldn't decide which would be worse: Teddy in a room with a tiger ... or alone in a room with Derrick Pierce. He continued to stare at the tiger feed, and on the other side of the room, the chair remained empty.

Realizing that, for the moment, there wasn't anything he could do about Teddy, he spent his time in captivity trying to work out what coded message he could send to Hedges, through the PIT reservation system.

Now that he knew what Hedges meant—about needing help—he had to at least *try* to do whatever he could with his limited ability to move, with his limited resources. With the tablet—

Just then, a new reservation request popped up.

B. ROSS: PIT-1>> SPIDER 84a >> 3:00 P.M.

Although Oscar had seen more than his share of unbelievable things that day, seeing Branson Ross at Pantheon was almost as bizarre as learning about the discovery of an alien social network.

In Oscar's recollection, Branson Ross was the only person in the world who'd ever bested Derrick Pierce.

Back in 2013, Branson and Pierce competed for the same NASA contract—a multibillion-dollar award to build and administer a new space station complex. A joint public-private venture, it would be a coup for whichever contractor won the bid.

After a hard-fought battle, Pantheon was declared the victor, but in short order, several memos were leaked to the press—memos hinting of bribes between Pierce and an unnamed Member of Congress.

When the news broke, there was a public outcry. But, nothing could be proven; the Department of Justice's investigation didn't turn up any more than the somewhat cryptic memos, and they couldn't determine who in Congress was implicated.

Nevertheless, NASA withdrew the contract from Pantheon and turned it over to Branson's company, the runner-up.

Pierce—unaccustomed to losing—never recovered from the public humiliation, and did everything in his power to undermine Branson at every turn, primarily by ensuring Pantheon was always the first-to-market with the latest technology, the latest must-have, gadget....

That was why Oscar was so surprised to see Branson participating in Pierce's "beta test". If Branson knew what Pierce was up to—

Of course!

Oscar's brain finally kicked in ... finally returned from its extended siesta.

Thanks, guy. A little down to the wire, but I'll take what I can get.

He swiped at the reservation screen, opened the Branson PIT request, made a slight adjustment, and said a small prayer his message would be understood.

CHAPTER 71

Hedges was putting the finishing touches on the flat version of Earth's immersion packet when he saw the new reservation request. It was a strange one.

B. ROSS: PIT-1>>FROG SOUP>>3:00 P.M.

"*Frog soup?* What the hell—"

He wondered if his addled brain had finally devolved into hallucinating. Maybe now he was a certifiable, raving nutter. Maybe they'd keep him locked underground forever. Images flashed through his mind. Images of stacks of white buckets and canned food and PIT chairs adorned with restraints....

He shook his head and peered at the reservation; it hadn't changed. He wasn't crazy; Branson Ross's request had to have been revised by Oscar.

Based on the security map of pheromone signatures, Hedges knew Oscar was in one of the PIT rooms; he would have a tablet and access to the reservation screen.

He was happy to discover that the guy was doing okay. At least, he'd been able to send a message—he must have *some* freedom of movement. But, what the hell did it mean?

FROG SOUP was in place of the planet name, so *what,* exactly, was Oscar trying to tell him? That he should load up FROG SOUP for Branson to view ... instead of an immersion? How was he to do *that?*

His mind was still churning over the meaning of the obscure reference, when Pierce commed from EB-II.

"So, can I review the damn thing ... or do you plan on sittin' there diddlin' yerself 'til we're good 'n past the deadline?"

Hedges's hackles rose, and—in a flash—he understood what FROG SOUP meant.

Oh my God! Why hadn't I thought of that? Thank you, Oscar!

"Kid, wake the fuck up! Is it ready?"

"No."

Click.

Hedges stood in the middle of the Edit Bay and looked out across the long expanse of the Grid room, hoping that Pierce was on his way there, and not on his way to Oscar or Teddy—

He was flooded with relief when he heard Pierce's footsteps.

Moments later, the Director stood just inside the Edit Bay door, hands on his hips, cigar clenched between his teeth. There was a small bandage above his left temple.

CHAPTER 72

Hedges, with the green light blinking in the corner of his eye, hoped the implant was functioning as designed. There wouldn't be time for a second take.

Pierce glowered.

Hedges glanced down, certain Pierce could see the blinking light ... that somehow, he could see he was being recorded. But that was impossible—

"If you think you're gonna convince me to open the Grid to the people and hand over the tech library, you can save your breath. We've been over that."

The Director began to pace, working himself into a lather, ready for another battle.

"Not at all. You're right."

Pierce looked startled by the sudden acquiescence. He stopped pacing and his eyes narrowed. "You sassin' me?"

"No, really ... I thought about it, and you're right; of *course* you should be the one to decide which of the technologies Earth would benefit from. I just wanted to go over how you want me to hide the tech library folder. You know, from users like Branson Ross, President deGrey, and users from other countries."

Pierce relaxed then, smirked, and waved his cigar in the air. "Just lock it behind that 'God Mode' whoozit. Only give me access. I ain't no genius, but it seems pretty simple to me...."

"Right, of course ... the 'God Mode' whoozit," Hedges couldn't resist, but when Pierce turned and eyed him, he smiled a benign smile and said, "That'll be easy enough. And what about the Grid portal ... and the immersion packets? Once the Gridmaster notices the people of Earth have stopped downloading immersions, it'll only be a matter of time before they investigate and delete our encryption key—"

"I been thinkin' about that. You said there are billions of years of tech archives, right? Probably stuff that can help you science geeks develop cancer-resistant DNA, life extension technologies, clean energy ... shit like that, right?"

"Yeah...."

"Well, I mean, what more do we really need? We have plenty of planet immersion packets we can turn into apps for the rest of the world to enjoy. Like you said ... we could modify Pantheon tablets and other handhelds ... we can still capitalize on the Grid and I'll have the full tech library. Genius!"

"You don't see the value in waiting to see what new planets are added ... what additional technologies there might be?"

Pierce chuckled. "Now who's bein' greedy? Billions of years of inventions ain't enough for ya?"

Hedges bit his tongue. He didn't have time for a philosophical debate.

"Look, I understand why you locked me down here this weekend. I get that you were just protecting the integrity of the project, but what about the deaths of Marvin Trimble and Senator Higgs? And, what do you plan do with Oscar Rand and Teddy Lawson?"

"The nerdlets are fine—or they will be as soon as you get with the program and do what you're told. As for the others, well, sometimes things need to be done ... it's the cost of doing business. Trimble only had a few months to live ... as for the Senator, well, he was a man of science, a futurist; I'm sure he'd have been proud to contribute to our little project."

Pierce looked at his watch. "Kid, I'm glad you finally came 'round to seeing things my way; we make a great team, my business sense and your brains ... but now, we need to move it along." He nodded at the wall of displays. "Load it up for me."

Hedges—confident he had as much as he would get—complied. He sat at the desk and copied the flat version of Earth's immersion packet to Pierce's folder.

Then, he steeled himself; he wasn't quite done with the plan, and the rest would be tricky. "You'll need to review it in the Ops Center."

"No, I'll look at it here. *You* can go to the Ops Center and wait for my instructions."

Hedges couldn't allow that. He needed to stay in the Edit Bay while Pierce was occupied. As it was, he'd barely have enough time to edit the confession before Branson's appointment.

He thought quickly. "I need to prep the messenger-Q to ensure that the Grid Relay receives the optimal state request—"

Pierce's face screwed up into a look of distaste. "What the hell ya babblin' about?"

"It'll be faster if I stay here and prep for final transmission. That way, when you're done with your review, I'll be here ... ready to send it off to the Grid."

He hoped it would work. What he'd told Pierce was bullshit—there was no need for any lead-time or prep work—but he was gambling that Pierce wouldn't be familiar with the Grid relay and entanglement transfer.

Pierce studied Hedges for a moment and again, Hedges looked away, sure his entire head was one big blinking green light.

Pierce frowned and again looked at his watch. "Fine, whatever; then, you better be good 'n ready ... standing by for my go. You've really let this get down to the wire." With that, he left.

CHAPTER 73

It was a small victory, but the FROG SOUP plan was far from done.

Branson Ross—with his animosity toward Pierce—would be the perfect target for the recorded confession, but recording it had been the easy part.

Somehow, Hedges would need to extract the recording, convert it to *n*bits, then get it queued up for Branson ... without Pierce noticing.

His only hope was that the Crazy Cowboy would be too wrapped up in viewing Earth's packet to notice what was going on in Edit Bay-I.

The recording had gone as well as could be expected, with Pierce admitting to his roles in the deaths of Senator Higgs and Marvin Trimble, as well as bragging about his future plans for the Grid.

It was a damning indictment, straight from the horse's mouth, and Branson would be the perfect audience. Hedges couldn't think of any other PIT user he would've trusted.

Even so, there was no way to predict how Branson would react....

Hedges sent a message back to Oscar, letting him know his idea was received, understood, and executed. Then, keeping his movements as minimal as possible, he reached into one of the desk drawers and pulled out a lockbox. Inside, was a handheld Onculus.

He placed the eye-shaped suction cup over his right eye and pressed a button on its side. A laser locked onto the implant and began to retrieve the new data.

So far so good, he thought, but then—when the laser had retrieved just 65 percent of the data—He was startled by a *click*.

He turned his head slowly toward the COMM monitor, and saw, with his unobstructed eye, the dreaded white text: OPS CENTER.

Shit!

Hedges—his hand shaking and his breathing erratic—tried to hold the Onculus as steadily as possible.

Was it a 2-way feed this time?

Could Pierce see him ... could he see the Onculus pressed to his eye?

"What's my password?"

Hedges took a deep breath and shakily rattled off the password, all the while, the laser continued to retrieve the data.

95 percent had been retrieved by the time Pierce noticed.

"Kid, what the hell ya doin'?"

Definitely 2-way.

Thinking fast, Hedges said, "Just making sure there's no residual data from our recording tour. We wouldn't want to miss anything...."

"Better not. We don't have time to diddle around with adding more; it took ya long enough to get the rest of it in there."

Click.

Hedges exhaled. Then, still shaking, he transmitted the neural recording from the Onculus to QUINN.

By the time Branson was scheduled to go into PIT-1, Hedges had finished the $n$bit conversion of the FROG SOUP packet and had uploaded it to Branson's queue.

He renamed it SPIDER 84a so Branson wouldn't notice anything amiss ... until he was already immersed.

Now, it was out of his hands—it was up to Branson to take action, based on what he saw. But would he? Would he care?

Unfortunately, by the time three o'clock rolled around, Hedges feared he'd never find out. He feared the entire FROG SOUP plan had been a colossal waste of time. Branson's appointment time came and went, with no sign of activity in PIT-1.

Hedges grew more and more anxious as the minutes ticked by. He stared at the PIT activity log and still, the queued-up Pierce confession sat in Branson's queue. Waiting.

CHAPTER 74

Pierce watched the last scene and wished, for the first time since his implant failure, that he still had the ability to do immersions.

Their packet had turned out even better than he'd hoped and he wouldn't be surprised if Earth's immersion soon had the highest ratings on the Grid....

He glanced down at his tablet and checked in on the kids. Hedges still waited patiently for him to finish, waited for instructions.

Good boy.

And, the poofy-haired kid was sitting in his PIT room, staring wall-eyed at the tiger video. He flipped over to the girl's feed; she was doing the same.

Love insurance, Pierce thought, was by far the most effective. It was something he'd never understand. Why would anyone put someone else's survival over their own? Why would they hand such power over to another human being? It made no sense....

Whatever. The tiger holograms were working as planned. They'd been a gift from some consultant, a while back—a gift for Pierce's birthday or boss's day or some other twaddle—the Agrippa nerdlets were always doing shit like that.

As he watched the hologram prowl and snarl, he smiled. He could have locked the two of them in Security, or taken them to the barracks, but the tiger was more entertaining.

CHAPTER 75

Hedges waited, still hoping that Pierce would be so wrapped up in Earth's packet, that he would stay away long enough for Branson to show up for his appointment.

But, his worst fears came true when, at around three thirty, Pierce finished, and PIT-1 remained empty.

Click.

COMM: OPS CENTER

"It's fine. Do the upload ... *now!*"

Pierce sounded like he expected pushback, but Hedges was out of moves ... had no more aces up his sleeve; he'd played his best and final card.

Now, if Hedges delayed the upload, it was be *his* fault if Earth was cut off....

"Yes, sir," he said, defeated.

And finally, but probably too late to do any good, there was activity in PIT-1.

Branson Ross had finally arrived.

Feeling sick, Hedges did the one thing Pierce had been waiting for. He requested a messenger-*Q* and sent Earth's immersion packet to the Grid.

CHAPTER 76

[TRANSLATION: GS15-CIRCINI-Ω>>EARTH-G-α5B-3215]
Hedges stood in the middle of the Grid room, in front of a hologram of Uri, the Senior Technician for Grid Sector 15.

Uri looked like a cross between an Oompa-Loompa and a Weeble: light orange, squat, pear-shaped body, no legs. He hovered in the air and bobbled up and down.

"Hedges, Earth's packet was one of the best I've ever seen."

As Uri spoke, his Circinian language was auto-translated.

"I bet you say that to all the planets," Hedges said. He was thrilled to be talking with Uri; happy to focus on something other than Pierce, if only for a moment.

Uri weebled. "No, it's true. I loved the adrenaline sensations of the FEAR option; we don't get to experience that here."

"You don't feel fear? Why not? I thought your brain morphology was nearly identical to ours?"

"Yes, but for Circinians, the adrenal gland is vestigial ... no adrenaline rushes here. My cortex was drowning in the stuff when we jumped off the bridge."

Hedges's stomach flipped. "Well, I'm glad *someone* enjoyed it. I must admit though, I'm even more curious to try *your* planet's packet, if only to see what it's like to be fearless...."

"Well, the good news is, you can do that now; Earth is a full user! Your packet has been approved by the Gridmaster and is now available, in fact, it's already been requested several million times. Very soon, you'll start to see reviews from other users."

"Several million times? Unbelievable...."

Uri pulled up an image of Earth's Grid file structure. Hedges could see that, below the packet library, the T-LIB was no longer grayed out, and the padlock icon was gone.

"Here's a look at your new directory," Uri said.

"Great," Hedges said, trying to sound enthusiastic. But what should have been one of the most important events in human history, was now shrouded in a dark pallor ... thanks to Derrick Pierce.

Hedges prayed that Branson would be out of the PIT room before Pierce could get his greedy mitts on the tech folder. And, Uri's next words gave him hope.

"As you can imagine, the amount of information contained in the tech library will take a while to propagate in your folders. But, look here," Uri zoomed into the Grid's file structure and opened one of the folders in the T-LIB. "You'll see that *your* planet's technologies have been added, based on the information you provided with your packet."

Hedges looked at the file folder. The one filled with thousands of years of human ingenuity.

He thought of Earth's inventions—the atomic bomb, the semiconductor, the steam engine, the space shuttle, the Hubble Telescope, bioengineered super-viruses and vaccines, the DNA sequence library for all Earth's species—and he couldn't help but wonder how sophomoric it would seem to more evolved, more advanced civilizations.

Would it be like sifting through the artwork of a toddler ... like browsing through amusing finger paintings and paper-chain turkeys?

He suspected it would. But maybe, just maybe, another civilization would find something useful within Earth's bag of tricks—

Hedges was pulled from his musings when Uri made a sound, like the clearing of a throat. "Make sure everyone on your planet—every one of its users—is given free access to all libraries and all content. Any restriction of any folder, for any reason, is a violation of the Grid's long-standing tradition of open-source information sharing."

"What about mass-extinction technologies? Do you filter out the more dangerous tech ... to prevent civilizations from destroying themselves?"

"No way," Uri said. "Everything goes in ... no exceptions. By the time a species has evolved to the point of finding a Grid beacon, and responding, surely they're enlightened enough to be trusted with potentially catastrophic tech. Besides, can you imagine editing that [undefined expletive]? Who has the time? Anyway, who should decide what's cataclysmic? What may be catastrophic for one civilization could mean salvation for another. But, again, evolution over billions of years makes intentional annihilation by natives probabilistically unlikely."

As Hedges listened to Uri speak of evolved and enlightened beings, he felt a mixture of guilt and anger.

Pierce was about to violate the trust of an entire universe—not to mention the trust of more than seven billion humans—and Hedges was doing precious little to stop him.

In contrast to Hedges's dark thoughts, Uri's mood was light. "And, in the off-chance a planet *does* manage to blow itself up, well, then, what can I say? Fewer planets mean less work for me."

That sent the Circinian into fits of laughter; his bulbous body shook and bobbled. He laughed so hard, he bobbled partly out of view.

Momentarily, he centered back into frame. "Anyway, we're running out of space on this gate. Do you have any other questions before I sign off?"

CHAPTER 77

Hedges asked, "How much of the Universe does GS15 cover?"

"All of it."

Hedges laughed.

"Uri, I think the translator failed," he said, and struggled to rephrase the question. "I mean, what fraction of the Universe, of all of the space," he waved his arms in wide sweeping gestures as he struggled to clarify *all the space*. "What fraction of all that does Sector 15 represent?"

Uri bobbled. "The translation was accurate and your confusion is understandable; you think of Sector 15 as a fraction of the Universe, but it's actually the whole of what your people have labeled the "Universe". On the Grid, a sector is just one of many such "universes". We don't really know how many sectors there are on the Grid. Earth and Circini-Omega are catalogued within Sector—or *Universe*—15. Either way, sector ... universe, it's all the same concept, just different labels and scope."

Shit, thought Hedges, *GS15 is one of a multiverse!*

"So, we can request immersion packets from ... say ... GS9?"

Uri weebled. "Not as far as we can tell. At least within GS15, downloads between sectors haven't been performed. We know they're there ... we can see their packet libraries, but we don't know how many sectors there are. As you can see," Uri said, and opened the Grid file directory—an endless list of folders—and he started the screen on a rapid scroll. "The GS files go on and on, well past GS2G. No way to sort by number; tried it once and froze the entire system—the one and only time GS15 went offline." He closed out of the directory, then continued.

"Other civilizations have tried to open other sector folders. One civilization—in GS15a214—has their entire population working on an exosector download. Story goes, it's been downloading for a hundred million years. Maybe someday, it'll finally open. Who knows? Strange thing is, there are no records of beacon responses from any of those sectors. So, which Grid technician added them to the central library, you might ask? We don't know. That's the fun part of my job; always something new. As you will soon see, the Grid is overflowing with weirdness.

"One theorist, in GS15a508, believes there's sector-hopping going on, but that GS15 is one of the slow kids—one of the sectors who hasn't figured out how to jump. If so, do those sectors wonder why GS15 isn't playing with the others? Why we aren't downloading and rating any of their immersions? Wouldn't that be something? They'd say: *"What? Was it something we said?"*

That sent Uri into another fit of bobbling and weebling laughter.

Hedges smiled and waited for the convulsions to subside; the intermission was a welcome respite, one his brain sorely needed. Uri had given him even more information to process on an already overwhelming day.

He'd been so wrapped up in QUINN for so long, first with the excitement of completing the array, then to finding the beacon and learning about the Grid, to the rapid devolution of Pierce's grip on reality, and finally to the present—to the tech library being unlocked....

It was refreshing to laugh, and to talk with a like mind. To contemplate what it was all about. Hedges didn't want it to end. He and Uri could have been any two colleagues anywhere, just shootin' the shit.

How messed up was it, that the first time he felt sane in months, was when he was talking to an alien?

It should have been depressing, Hedges thought, to realize that—after peering beyond the visible universe, beyond one limited field of view—there was another field of view, even more mysterious than the previous.

And, it was then you realized there were just more questions, more hypotheticals ... more theories. It should have been unsettling—should have crushed him with a profound sense of futility—but Hedges found it oddly comforting. Not only were they not alone—physically—but they were not alone in questioning the mysteries of the Universe—the Multiverse. The state of unknowing was *literally* universal. Seemingly infinite.

Finally, Uri regained his composure and said, "Anyway, GS15 is growing fast, so fast I don't have time to worry about the other sectors. Which reminds me; there's another matter I wanted to discuss...."

Then, Uri made Hedges a startling offer.

CHAPTER 78

From Edit Bay-II, Pierce watched as the alien meeting wrapped up.

He was happy he didn't have to sit through that; after the first few live feeds with the orange geek, it was clear to him that alien nerdlets were just as tedious as the ones he had on Earth.

No matter. He'd heard the one thing he needed to hear—the tech library was open! After the day's comedy of errors, it was a goddamn miracle....

He glanced at the T-LIB file.

After so many months of staring at that blasted padlock, it was finally gone. Underneath the folder, there was a progress bar showing how much of the library had been downloaded. For Pierce, it was like watching a bank transfer in progress. One that would never stop giving.

Keeping an eye on the progress bar, he continued on with his other work. Work that had been constantly interrupted with nonsense from the kids.

So many interruptions, he'd begun to feel like he was running a day-care center instead of a corporation. Finally though, he'd been able to get Hedges to see things his way.

It shouldn't have taken so long for the kid to realize Pierce had everyone's best interest at heart. After everything he'd done for the boy—the limitless opportunities he'd given him ... all the time and money spent mentoring the kid. He'd even intended to give Hedges control of Earth's entire Grid operation, for however long Earth's access remained ... maybe he still would.

But, now wasn't the time for such things. He needed to be sure nobody else got their grubby hands on his tech.

He closed out of his INSURANCE file and left the room. On the way back to the Ops Center, Pierce read the names on the PIT room displays. One in particular stood out: Branson Ross, in PIT-1.

That shitheel may have managed to wrangle the space station contract, but now, that'll be Junior League next to the tech toys Pantheon was about to crank out.

The next few weeks, months, and years would be filled with patent filings and manufacturing. Pierce would need to build many more facilities like Agrippa.

He tugged at his shirt cuffs. He was moments away from taking his rightful place in history; for decades, he'd been on top—on Earth—and God continued to smile, ready to reward him for his vision and hard work....

He swiped at his touchpad, commed the kid, and told him to hightail it to the Ops Center.

CHAPTER 79

Oscar stared at the reservation screen.

RES LOG/B. ROSS: PIT-1>>SOUP'S ON>>IN
PROGRESS

His initial relief at seeing the updated PIT appointment was replaced by anxiety when he saw the IN PROGRESS notation.

He glanced at the clock in the corner of the screen. It was wrong. The date underneath the clock read 9/19/2015. It should read *10/5*/2015, also, the clock indicated it was noon, but Oscar knew that couldn't be right.

It had to be past Branson's appointment time—had to be after three o'clock. He needed to find out how *far* past. According to Hedges, Earth's immersion packet was due by 4:00 P.M., and last time he checked, it was—

He dug into his pocket and pulled out his cell phone. He pressed the button on the side. A red battery icon appeared, but just for a moment, then the screen went blank.

Perfect. Dead battery.

He started to put it back in his pocket, when he saw something he'd never noticed. There it was, on the back, in worn, raised letters: Another fine product of Pantheon Holdings.

Oscar rolled his eyes, but wasn't surprised. He *tried* to buy fair-trade, but it was almost impossible to find personal technology devices without some component linked to Pantheon, one way or another.

He looked up at the wall display.

The tiger was in the snarl phase of its routine, and before Oscar could think—before he could think he might destroy his only connection to Teddy—he hurled the phone at the display.

The display must have been made of DuraBrane, because, after striking the tiger, the phone merely bounced back and clattered to the floor.

He scowled at the screen and the tiger snarled back.

Shaking his head, Oscar turned his attention back to the tablet. He tapped on the erroneous clock and a menu appeared.

He swiped at the SYNCH icon—to link it to atomic time—and was prompted for an Administrator password.

With growing frustration, he flipped back to the PIT room status. The message hadn't changed.

RES LOG/B. ROSS: PIT-1>>SOUP'S ON>>IN
PROGRESS

Were they too late? Did Pierce already have the tech library? Oscar felt helpless and blind, not knowing what was going on outside.

But he couldn't move. He couldn't do anything to jeopardize Teddy. He stared at the tiger feed, stared at the empty chair—

That's odd.

He peered at the feed. There it was again; a jitter on the tiger's left flank. The stripes shifted and, behind the tiger, he could see part of the Pantheon logo. Then, the stripes reappeared.

It was the same video artifact he'd seen while in the middle of the intergalactic Grid.

The tiger was a hologram!

Oscar strained forward to get a better look at the feed, a better look at the side of the room with the empty chair. He realized then the chair and carpet were identical to the ones in his own PIT room.

Then, he saw a similar jitter on the wrought iron, and he was convinced the entire scene was a composite of a tiger hologram and one of the PIT rooms.

He wondered if Teddy was still at Pantheon, wondered if she was okay....

Now, less fearful of moving, Oscar got out of the chair. He stretched, his muscles ached from tension and from remaining in the chair for so long.

He stood still, next the chair, half-expecting there to be an explosion, or an alarm, *something* ... but nothing happened. Nervous but determined, he went to the door and turned the knob. The door opened smoothly and he glanced out into the hallway. It was quiet. Empty.

He stepped one foot into the hall, then heard the unmistakable *clomp, clomp, clomp* of cowboy boots. He smelled cigar smoke....

Oscar's heart pounded and he ducked back into the room. He rushed back to the chair and sat down, certain the door would open at any moment.

The clomping grew louder until it stopped just outside the door. Then, to Oscar's relief, the footsteps started up again and Doppler-shifted away.

Pierce was gone.

There had been no other footsteps accompanying the cowboy boots, so he must have been alone. Not with Teddy.

Oscar wanted to tear out of there. He needed to find her, to make sure she was okay, but he knew the smartest move—at least until Branson Ross was done with his immersion—would be to sit tight and hope their plan worked.

He glanced at Branson's PIT room status and decided to wait a few more minutes. After that, all bets were off.

He'd sooner die than allow that sick twist to harm a single hair on Teddy's head.

CHAPTER 80

Hedges shuffled down the hall with footsteps as heavy as his heart.

Pierce had returned before Branson; it was over. What more could he do?

His dismal mood was in stark contrast to the sense of wonder he'd felt while talking with Uri, while discussing the Universe, while discussing cooperative sharing with enlightened beings, while talking of boundless possibilities.

He trudged past PIT-1 and saw Branson's name, still scrolling across the display; if Branson didn't hurry, his plan would've been all for naught.

And, what if he *did* come out in time—before the tech library finished downloading? Would he care about Pierce's admission, about his plans to destroy Earth's connection to the Grid?

Maybe Hedges and Oscar had given Branson too much credit; maybe Branson had a side deal with Pierce to hoard the Grid tech....

As he approached the Ops Center, he saw Pierce lounging at the desk, boots kicked up, puffing on a cigar. To Hedges, he'd never looked more self-satisfied....

When Hedges walked in, Pierce dropped his feet and sat forward, eager.

"Giddy up kid; molasses on a hot sidewalk moves faster than you. Sign into the library. And it better be set so I'm the only one that can see the damn thing."

Pierce was annoyingly cheerful—seemingly oblivious to the terror he'd caused Hedges, Oscar, and Teddy. Not to mention what had befallen Marvin and Higgs. For Pierce, all was right in the world.

For Pierce, it was Christmas Day.

Hedges, with his mouth fixed in a straight line, signed into the Grid library. Underneath the T-LIB file, he saw that the progress bar was nearly halfway across.

Pierce grinned and turned to Hedges. He stared for a while. Then, he stubbed the cigar out on the bottom of his boot and tossed the smoldering, chewed-up stump onto the desk. He stood and tugged at his shirt cuffs.

Hedges recognized the look; it meant that Pierce had made some sort of decision.

"I had high hopes for you, kid, but this is where we part ways."

Pierce tapped on his tablet—on the security COMM icon—and said, "Reggie, get in here."

Hedges snapped, his blood boiled and his head buzzed. Maybe it was the smug look or because he'd been caged up down there, like an animal. Had been badgered and harangued and hovered over for months. Had been pushed to do things that stressed his neurons and his psyche. Maybe it was the way that, now that Pierce had what he wanted, he casually dismissed Hedges, and expected there to be no consequences for any of his actions.

Reasons didn't matter. At that moment, Hedges was the most dangerous kind of animal. One with nothing left to lose.

He lunged at Pierce, catching him off guard. Hedges was taller and stronger and managed to pin Pierce against the wall.

Pierce let his body go slack, and Hedges instinctively dropped his guard, loosened his grip just enough for Pierce to regain the upper hand.

With lightning-fast movements, Pierce regained control. Now, Hedges was pinned to the wall, with Pierce's forearm banded like steel against his windpipe.

Hedges gawped and choked. He stared into Pierce's eyes and saw the same dispassionate caclulation he'd seen while falling backward off the Bloukrans Bridge.

Cool … detached.

And Hedges thought, *Of course, this would be the way it would end.*

He'd die there in the underground without having seen the sun for days, like some mole person in a subway tunnel. He'd die without getting to explore the rest of the Universe; without getting to witness a changing Earth.

He wouldn't get to see a planet where every being had access to clean water and lived in sanitary conditions. Wouldn't get to see an Earth with low infant mortality, or one which ran on clean, sustainable energy....

He'd see none of that.

As he grew more lightheaded, he realized that all he'd see during the last moments of his life were those bottomless, calculating eyes.

But then, just before he slipped into darkness, he no longer felt pressure at his throat, on his chest.

His eyes snapped open just in time to see Pierce fly backward, as though he were being sucked into a vortex.

Then, he heard Branson's voice.

CHAPTER 81

"Derrick, we aren't roughnecks in an oilfield. Have some manners."

Branson had plucked Pierce off of Hedges and was holding him back with his arms pinned to his sides.

Pierce wrenched himself out of Branson's grasp and muttered, "Butt out Branson; it's none o' yours." He smoothed down his rumpled suit jacket and pouted.

"I disagree. I've just seen something that tells me this is very much my concern," Branson said, looking and sounding like he was scolding a petulant child.

It was an odd sight for Hedges, who couldn't recall the last time he'd seen someone get the best of Derrick Pierce. No. That wasn't quite true. The last time was also at the hands of Mr. Ross....

Pierce sneered. "What're you talkin' about?"

"I heard you say you planned to tell users this was all just a simulation ... and that you don't care if Earth loses its Grid connection. And, I learned there's a treasure trove of technology—a library you planned on keeping locked down, locked away from me and from the rest of the world. I heard you admit you played a role in the deaths of Marvin Trimble and Senator Higgs. It's unconscionable, Pierce, even for you."

"Oh? And how—pray tell—did you hear all that? You get someone to spy on me?" Pierce glanced out at the hall, out at Reggie and the other security detail.

Branson shook his head, looking grim. "I've been in the PIT, watching a packet, but not one from the Grid. I had gone in expecting to be immersed in a planet where beings lived in peace and harmony; instead, I had to watch the most sickening display of avarice and hubris I'd ever seen. Don't get me wrong, I'm thankful to Trey here, for having the courage to let us know what was going on behind our backs."

Branson turned and nodded at Hedges. "Thank you, son. A fine job."

Hedges took that as his cue. He picked up a tablet, and navigated to his file directory. He tapped on FROG SOUP and Pierce's voice filled the room.

Every display on the curved wall showed the flat versions of the packet Branson had viewed.

"Well, I mean, what more do we really need? We have plenty of planet immersion packets we can turn into apps for the rest of the world to enjoy. Like you said ... we could modify Pantheon tablets and other handhelds ... we can still capitalize on the Grid and I'll have the full tech library. Genius!"

While it played, Hedges felt hope for the first time in many months. He was gratified to see their faith in Branson hadn't been misplaced, and he couldn't resist rubbing salt in Pierce's wounds. He wanted it to hurt....

"I made a little add-on packet in which you were the star; Mr. Ross was the first to preview it."

"You recorded *me*?"

On Pierce's face, Hedges saw the reaction he expected—anger and irritation—but it was quickly replaced by something else, something unexpected: amusement.

Before Hedges could identify the source of Pierce's amusement, another voice came in from the hall.

"It's all over, Derrick."

CHAPTER 82

"What the—" Pierce stared as several dozen PIT users filed into the Ops Center and lined up around the curved walls.

Among them, Hedges recognized Prime Minister Landham and Gloria Turing. Also, Donald Ponzelli, Chairman of the Federal Reserve.

Branson addressed Pierce. "We just had an impromptu meeting. I filled them in on your plans. Told them you believe the Grid and the intellectual property of the Universe is yours to do with as you wish."

Pierce, who had initially been startled by their appearance, recovered quickly.

Too quickly for Hedges's liking. He expected Pierce to be losing the rest of what little marbles he had upon realizing the jig was up—that his crazy-town rodeo was over—but Pierce seemed calm. Amused.

"You think the world is better off if ya'll run it without me? Without my money, my connections, without Agrippa?"

Turing, a senior board member, stepped forward and said, "None of it belongs to you. Not anymore; it belongs to Pantheon Holdings, remember? And, since you've violated your contract with the stakeholders—not to mention the assurances you gave each of us—we've unanimously agreed that Branson Ross should take over as interim Director. And, all Pantheon assets will be placed in a trust."

Pierce shrugged and smiled, "Well now, Gloria, sweetie, before you go and do that—and by all means, ya'll are free to do as you see fit—but seein' as we're all here, why don't we take a look at some videos?" Smirking, he picked up his tablet.

He turned and looked at the Fed Chair. "Donnie, old pal, how was your meeting in Geneva? You know ... the one with Mun Kim Phak?

The blood drained from Ponzelli's face and Hedges wondered, as most everyone in the room was probably wondering, what the Chairman of the Federal Reserve would be doing meeting with a sworn enemy of the state.

"I know, I know," Pierce continued. "You thought nobody knew about that, right? I gotta admit, you covered your tracks well, but I saw what *you* saw ... it was like I was standin' right there with you—like I was inside your head, watching everything."

Ponzelli looked confused. And afraid. "What are you talking about? You've been *spying* on us?"

"No, you've been spyin' on yourselves," Pierce looked around the room and waited for the implication of his words to sink in.

Hedges thought he understood what Pierce was trying to say, but he knew it was an empty claim. Pierce had to be bluffing.

Some had begun to understand what Pierce was getting at, still others looked confused.

"Ya see, there's this nifty little option in each implant, tucked away behind somethin' my boy Hedges likes to call 'God Mode'—"

At that, Hedges was happy to jump in and expose Pierce's bluff. "Not possible. Implants won't record unless the user gives the command. That option isn't enabled in any of your implants ... only in mine. Besides, not every brain's suitable for recording; in the wrong user, recording could lead to permanent brain damage—or death...."

Pierce waved away the interruption as though waving away a horsefly. He continued to address the room. As he spoke, he looked more and more pleased with himself.

"Doc and I tweaked a few implants, gave 'em a remote-start option. No pesky blinking lights to signal when they're recording." He smiled and nodded toward the displays and looked at each person in the room. "Now, should we all have a look and see what my users have been up to? Or should we forget this ever happened."

Hedges watched while the power elite frantically searched the recesses of their minds, trying to recall their activities of the past few days, weeks, and months.

Most of them—Hedges knew—had been at the Geneva Summit the night before, an annual event with many opportunities for dealings in darkened backrooms—the sort of dealings that wouldn't hold up well under the harsh light of public scrutiny.

Branson stepped forward and said, "Go ahead, Derrick. Do your worst ... I have nothing to hide."

Pierce sneered. "Well, that's mighty white o' ya, Branson, but you're not in my little video library, are ya? Too soon for you. And, yeah, you're probably right ... your videos would be a snooze-rodeo. As for the rest of your buddies, well, let's just say I've managed to put together an interesting collection...."

CHAPTER 83

Hedges flashed back to all the times he'd seen Pierce sneak in and out of Edit Bay-II. Now, he knew why that activity had burrowed in his mind and sat—just out of reach—like an itch he couldn't scratch. Waiting.

He'd never thought Pierce had paid the slightest attention to the tutorial on packet recording and conversion. He knew Pierce wasn't the Luddite he pretended to be, but to remote record and edit packets? If Hedges hadn't been so horrified, he'd have been impressed....

Pierce must have performed backend retrievals when the users went in for immersions. Then, he would have edited flat conversions—sidestepping the qubit conversion.

Flat versions of Pierce's surveillance would still be effective. Effective enough to scare the group in the Ops Center into a panicked cooperation with Pierce's continued domination and control.

It was *because* the users were powerful men and women—with all manner of secrets—that they had made it onto Derrick Pierce's exclusive list. If they didn't harbor the sort of secrets that could be used to make one person owe another many years of favors, they would've been no use to Pierce—

Ponzelli, looking comically like the Monopoly banker, with his three-piece suit, bald head, and bushy mustache—but minus the cane—stepped forward. He held his hands out to Pierce and said, "Let's not be hasty. You don't want to make this any worse for all of us, do you? I'm sure we can come to an understanding...." His voice shook slightly and there was a twitch in the corner of his left eye.

It was obvious the last thing the Fed Chair wanted was for his personal clips to be aired, in front of his peers.

From the nods and the assenting murmur rippling throughout the room, Hedges could see Ponzelli had plenty of support.

Pierce grinned. His smile said it all: game, set, and match. "Well, Branson, looks like you're outgunned." Smug, he set the tablet down and turned his back to the wall of displays. The cursor blinked patiently in the password field, waiting for 'dpierce' to sign in.

Hedges's unfocused eyes stared, the user login screen blurred and wavered. The cotton haze in his head was now steel wool and he felt sick.

If Pierce had insurance against all these powerful people, then things would continue on as they always had. He'd be untouchable; he'd get what he wanted from the tech library and the puppets would continue to do his bidding.

It was too much to bear—

But then, Hedges finally honed in on the blinking cursor, the one in the password field, and realized what it meant. He'd been staring at it, but hadn't seen.

Now, though, the way out was clear. Hedges knew Earth's Grid access would be safe. Everyone would be free from Pierce's oppression. Finally, the Crazy Cowboy had run out of insurance.

A wave of relief washed over Hedges and he threw his head back and laughed. He laughed until tears streamed down his face.

He knew that everyone in the room was staring at him like they were staring at a loon. They'd probably think that working for Derrick Pierce had finally sent him right 'round the bend.

After all, what would Hedges have to be happy about? But he *did* have something to be happy about.

Finally, he did....

He swiped at his eyes, got his laughter under control, and moved to stand in the middle of the room. He stood tall and gestured toward the login screen.

In a loud voice, he said, "Actually, *Derrick*, why don't you go ahead and show us your videos? Sign in and access your files."

The Fed Chair jumped forward to silence Hedges. "Son, why don't you just let it alone?"

Hedges shook his head and smiled, "Don't worry, your secrets are safe; they'll be locked away for all eternity, isn't that right, Derrick?"

Pierce dropped into the chair in front of the desk and looked from Hedges to the login screen. Slowly, he got it: the one thing he needed—his best and final insurance—was unattainable.

The former Pantheon Director forced a smile and tried to pour on the charm. "Come on, kid; we'll run this thing together. Think of all we can do: my money, your brains ... you and me. Now go on and put in my password."

There was a collective release of tension throughout the Ops Center as everyone realized that Hedges was right; their secrets would remain locked away—

Just then, there was a loud *Ding!* and the background screen maximized on the center display. The T-LIB folder glowed green.

It was open for viewing.

Pierce lunged toward the touchpad but Reggie stepped in and pushed him back into the chair.

Hedges suddenly felt the eyes of everyone in the room and he realized they were waiting for guidance of some sort.

Did they think he was going to blackmail them with Pierce's surveillance? Is that why they were looking to him? What did they expect *him* to do?

But he surprised himself. He began to delegate, as though he'd been doing it all his life.

"Doc Thompson will be taken into custody, but his last task will be to ensure all implants are checked out. Then—only after everyone's been cleared—we'll meet back in the auditorium. We'll have another Grid orientation, but this time, it'll be a live broadcast, and will include a worldwide, tech library viewing party!"

And, to his surprise, everyone did as instructed.

As the users filtered out of the room, Pierce remained in his chair. He looked up at Hedges, his eyes drawn and beseeching.

Hedges looked with pity upon the man he'd once considered a great visionary. Pierce's suit was rumpled and he looked like he'd aged twenty years in 20 minutes.

CHAPTER 84

As the minutes ticked by, Oscar waited in the PIT room, his body coiled, wound like a spring. He had no idea what time it was.

Finally, he could wait no longer. He tore out of the PIT room and ran toward the Ops Center. He barely noticed the large group of people filing out of the room. He had only one target. One purpose.

He shoved past everyone and lunged toward Pierce, causing Hedges to jump out of his way.

"Where's Teddy, you sadistic prick?!" Oscar loomed over Pierce. He grabbed him by the lapels and shook him. Pierce's head flopped like a bobble-head doll, and he kept muttering, "What's my password? Kid, do you know my password?"

"Where's Teddy?!" Oscar yelled, and shook him again—

"Oscar!"

He heard her voice and the sound of footsteps running down the hall.

"Teddy!" He dropped Pierce and scrambled out of the Ops Center, into the hall. His heart crashed against his chest.

Dear God, let her be okay.

Then he saw her, running toward him. She barreled into his arms and clung to his shoulders.

She whispered in his ear, "That tiger in your room, oh my God ... are you hurt?"

Oscar shook his head and crushed her in his arms. He couldn't speak. Later, he would tell her all about the tiger hologram. He would tell her about the Grid. Later.

For the moment, there was only Teddy.

He leaned back and stared at her. He stroked her face, brushed the hair from her eyes and before he could stop himself, he kissed her.

And, it didn't take him long to realize, Teddy was kissing him back.

Branson stayed behind with Pierce. He nodded toward Reggie, who moved forward, handcuffs ready.

"What's my password?"

Branson slapped him on the back. "Don't worry, Derrick. I'm sure they'll give you a new password in prison. Might wanna write it down this time."

EPILOGUE

"Good morning, GS Tech Hedges."

"Good morning, GS Tech Rand."

"Where's Branson?"

"Ribbon-cutting in Tokyo. Opening of the millionth PIT franchise—"

"Oh right. Whatchya workin' on?"

Hedges glanced over his shoulder and said, "Browsing yesterday's tech." Then he turned back to the Grid library hologram.

The penthouse office had been gutted and redecorated, but the Sundance Colt remained, nestled between a pool table and a Q-bert game.

"Anything good?"

"It's *all* good ... and so obvious, when you get down to it."

"Occam's razor...."

"Isn't that always the way?"

They fell silent then, and worked.

Around lunchtime, the silence was interrupted by a *click*, and COMM: LOBBY appeared over the middle of the hologram.

"Hey, numbnuts!"

"Um ... your wife's here."

"Great!" Oscar said. "Time for lunch ... you comin'?"

"Yeah—wait, hang on; I think we're getting an alert. Yep, here it is: 3270 locked themselves out ... again."

"3270? In Alpha Centauri?"

"Yep."

"Noobs."

About the Author

Tesla Tao is a native of the Pacific Northwest and has been—at one time or other—a newspaper carrier, degenerate gambler, cryptographer, expatriate, NASA contractor, bartender, medical test subject, and writer.

Tao's subject matter is derived from a lifelong interest in technology, astronomy, neuroscience, information systems, genetics, psychology, and human behavior.